AF437815

The Secret Heir

A Class Source Novel

Written By
Kelly Beilfuss
Lydia Freeman
Chloe Windsor

A project of the 2020-2021 Novel Writing Class at Class Source of Tampa.
Instructed by Emily Fertic

Proceeds from the sale of this novel go toward Class Source Scholarships

Table of Contents

Dedications

I dedicate this to King Bob, for being the best little writing buddy and serenading me while I worked, and to the Lord above, who blessed me with the creativity and talent to be able to do this in the first place.

-Kelly Beilfuss

This year I want to dedicate this book to my friend Lilly. You really have made my school year. It took four previous introductions for us to actually interact, but once we did... Astivar. Need I say more? Anyway now that I have thanked you I must turn my gratitude towards my friend, now teacher, Emily Fertic, who was so incredible, I can't even tell you guys. This class is hard as a student, but teaching it is a whole other ball game and she crushed it. Also, once again, to my family for getting me a laptop for my last birthday; this class was so much easier.

-Lydia Freeman

I would like to dedicate this to my dad and siblings. Thank you for making life worth living.

-Chloe Windsor

Acknowledgements

To our beta readers — Beth Burnett, Crystal Crawford, Rachel Freeman, Valerie Garth, MJ Padgett, Lilly Ray, and Gracie Sanchez — thank you so much for your helpful feedback and willingness to help. Your comments were invaluable to all of us during the editing process whether they pointed out flaws or just made us laugh.

To our editor/proofreader extraordinaire, Christy Freeman. Just knowing that you were going to come behind and catch all of the little mistakes that I missed, took a lot of stress off of my shoulders. This is the fourth year in a row that you have so kindly volunteered to help edit a Class Source Novel and that kindness does not get overlooked. This book wouldn't be what it is without your help. Thank you.

To our cover wonderful cover artist, Dustin Goolsby. Every year since the beginning of this class, you have done something to help us out. Whether that meant designing a book cover or pretending to be a farmer fawning over his goats and wrapping about plants. You have donated your time and incredible talent yet again to make us another beautiful cover and we could not be more grateful. Thank you.

To our cartographer, Jaden Erickson. When I asked you for tips on map making because my students wanted to make a map for their book, you volunteered to make one for them. I told you that we couldn't pay you for it but you offered to do it anyway. Now, we have a beautiful map to go in the book and my students get to see the world they created, illustrated in a way that only a professional could do. Thank you for that gift.

To the Class Source community, thank you for your continued enthusiasm in your support of each year's novel. It always means so much to the students to see their book being supported that way.

To our readers, thank you again for joining us on this wild ride and joining us in the world of Aeternum.

Foreword

If this is your first time picking up a Class Source Novel, then first and foremost let me say thank you, for being a part of this and taking a chance on a student-written book.

The Class Source Novel is an annual project in which a group of middle and high school students collaboratively plan, write, edit, and indie-publish a novel over the course of a 32-week program year. All proceeds from the sales of the book go toward creating student scholarships for future writing classes.

This is my first year as instructor but I'm not new to the class. I was a student of this class for three years and am a co-author of the first three Class Source Novels. After I graduated, I couldn't bring myself to leave the class or the magic that comes with it. That's why I came back as an assistant to the former instructor, Crystal Crawford. I spent two years helping new groups of students produce their own novels from scratch and offering my perspective as someone who had been in their shoes. When Crystal decided to take a step back from teaching and offered me the class, I was elated and couldn't wait to start.

Every year we start from literally nothing… I'm serious. When the students and I step into the classroom on the very first day, none of us have any idea what we'll end up with by the end of the hour. That first day of class is equal parts nerve wracking and exhilarating. Most years, a good percentage of the students don't even know each other. Yet, by signing up for this class, they blindly agree to write a novel with what could be a group of total strangers. As the instructor, it's my job to lead this group of writers through the process of *collaboratively* brainstorming and deciding on a story genre and premise, and creating characters, a plot, and an outline. That's only the beginning, though. After that comes the process of writing and editing the novel that they've created together. The whole project requires immense teamwork and deep collaboration to just be completed-- let alone done well -- but they rose to the challenge.

I am so incredibly proud of my students. This class is not easy. In fact, the first day of class is traditionally filled with "let's hit you with the reality of this class now so that if you aren't up to it you can bow out now" speeches. The reality is that this class is *hard*. When you talk about writing a book most people's reactions are, "Oh I could never do that." Group projects are a near universally hated part of school life. These students *willingly* signed up for a year long group project of writing a novel. They crushed it. Every one of them not only finished their chapters and turned them in on time but they also met -- or exceeded -- their minimum word count every week. Each of them did their part in the editing process and even volunteered to do extra editing when it was needed. I have loved watching them learn new techniques to grow as writers and hone their craft. They all exhibited such dedication, maturity, and responsibility this year and I couldn't be more proud.

To my students: I know you all put everything you had into this book. You stuck it out through all of the "scary" speeches, late nights meeting word counts, and weeks of seemingly endless rounds of editing. Despite all of that, you faced every challenge head on with strength and maturity. You did it. You wrote a novel! How does it feel? I am so proud of you. Thank you, for being such a wonderful first class.

To the person reading this right now: Thank you. The proceeds from these books go toward producing scholarships for future writing classes and we appreciate that. But most of all, thank you for supporting these young writers in their goals and their visions for this book. For those that want to pursue writing as a career in the future, that support means the world. Thank you for joining them in this world that they've created and coming along with them on this adventure. We can't wait for you to read it.

Happy reading.

Sincerely,
Emily Fertic
Novel Writing Instructor

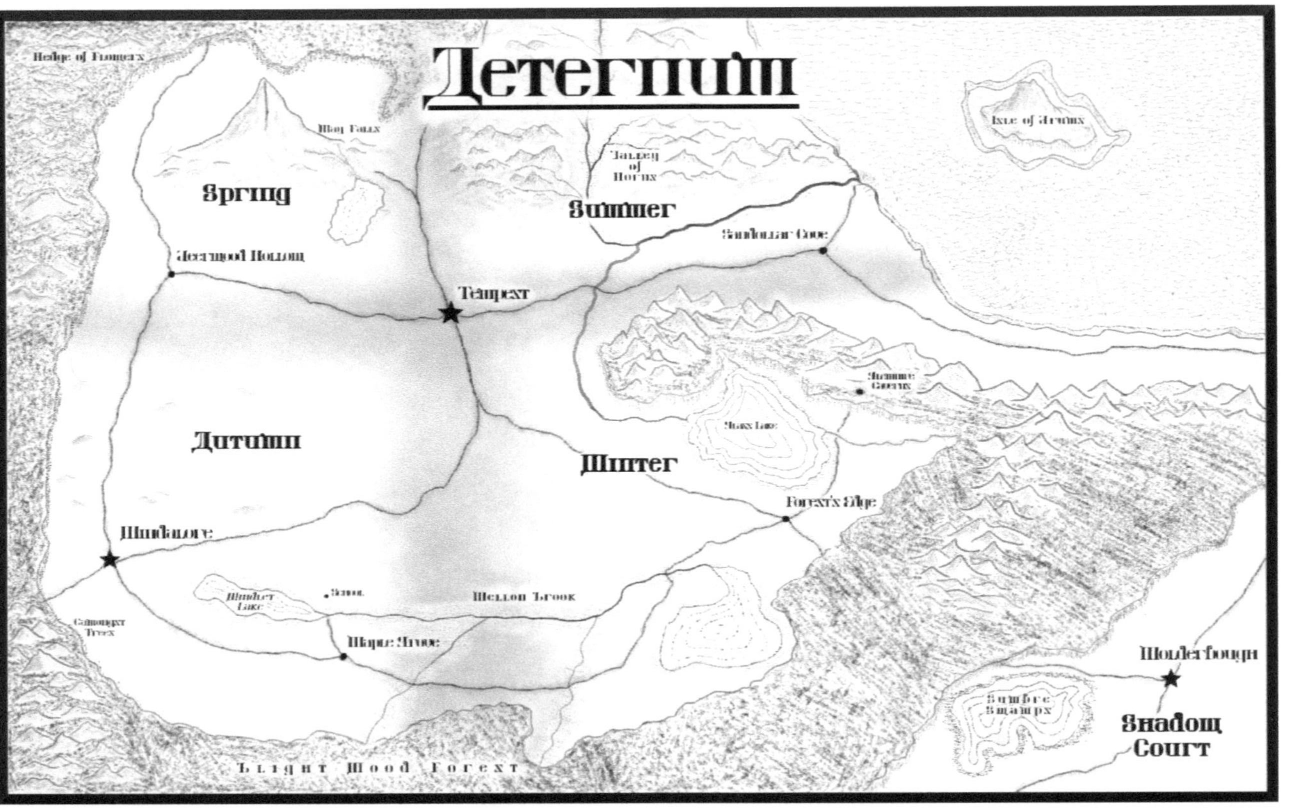

Aeternum
Hedge of Flowers
May Falls
Spring
Meerwood Hollow
Tempest
Valley of Horns
Summer
Sunflower Cove
Isle of Arrows
Winter
Summit Grotto
Mara's Lake
Forest's Edge
Autumn
Windgrove
Glinder Lake
Scout
Mellon Brook
Maple Grove
Cannoneer Trees
Twilight Wood Forest
Sombre Swamps
Shadowborough
Shadow Court

The Secret Heir

Chapter One

Evan stood next to the casket. His throat burned and his body trembled, he wanted to look away, but he couldn't stop staring at the lifeless face of his grandfather. In all the time he had known him he had never once seen his grandpa lay down, and to see him in that position, even in death, felt wrong somehow. Watery light streamed in through the clouds of the overcast sky and through the church's stained glass windows. Evan recoiled as the bright rays pierced his exhausted eyes. People milled around him patting his little sister on the head as she ran between their legs. Plodding on, they continued talking and exchanging stories, even an occasional laugh permeated the room. Evan didn't understand how they could laugh or smile. Still staring at his grandfather's casket, Evan's body began to shake. His face felt permanently downcast, any attempt to smile would only end in tears and he refused to make his mother watch that. She was dealing with the death of her father; the last thing she needed was for her son to break down completely. He knew his mom and if he lost his cool, she would put on a brave face for him, and she shouldn't have to do that. Vaguely, he realized someone was trying to say hello to him. He grit his teeth and tore his gaze away from the open casket. The person in front of him was a rather prunish woman that Evan guessed to be in her late sixties. He had the hazy impression that he was supposed to know her but he couldn't place her face, and was too emotionally spent to try.

"Hello Evan dear, how are you doing?" She said, coming in for a hug as she did so. Her cardigan sweater was itchy, and Evan's nose was besieged by her pungent perfume. Hesitantly he returned the embrace. *Why does everybody ask that?* He said something neutral because trying to say something pleasant made him want to punch a wall.

"About as well as you'd expect."

"Well if you need anything let me know," she responded, patting him on the shoulder before walking away. Looking to his left he saw his mom clutching her cousin tightly, both were sniffling, and hugging onto their legs was Noel. He saw her open her mouth to say something and he quickly took a step forward and scooped her up.

"Evan, what did you do that for?" She complained.

"Because Mom wants to hang out with her cousin and I wanted a 'Noel Hug'", Evan replied. This response seemed to placate her.

"I do give the best hugs, don't I?" she stated, assuming a very pleased look.

"The best, now can I receive one of your superior hugs?" Evan requested, her response to his praise causing the first twitch of a smile he'd had all day. Smiling, she opened her arms and threw them around her brother. Shoving her face into his chest she squeezed as hard as she could. Evan returned the pressure and laid his face on the top of her head. Evan didn't know how long he stood there holding on to his sister. *She probably won't even remember him in a few years.* This thought made him clutch her tighter until his knuckles were almost white.

"Evan, it's time to sit down," his Mom called. Noel squirmed in his grasp, and reluctantly, he set her on the ground and headed toward the front row. Sitting straight on the hard backed pew, he looked toward the podium. On it was an old man with puffy white hair and ruddy cheeks that were covered in wrinkles.

"Today, we are here to mourn the loss of a father, grandfather, veteran, and dear friend." He choked slightly on the latter. "As you know, James Robert Coreman was all of these..." The man warbled on. Hard as he tried, Evan couldn't focus on what the man was saying. All his attention was stuck on the man's appearance. There was nothing extraordinary about what he wore, a simple worn black suit and tie, and there was a wheezing tone to his voice. But a sense of familiarity and significance nagged at Evan's mind. He stared harder, squinting slightly. The bright light glinted off of something around the speaker's neck, the reflection pierced Evan's eyes and it hit him. *Uncle Charlie? But you weren't in the military, why do you have dog tags on?* His curiosity outweighed his fatigue, so he widened his eyes, attempting to regain his usual attentiveness.

"Acghem, excuse me." He cleared his throat and straightened the papers in his hand. "Dear Jim, when you, Jack and I met we were children, we didn't know what our future held, but we were determined to give our Kentucky backwater town a new definition of mischief." A collective chuckle went through those assembled, including Evan. "I still remember the days we were inseparable, but most of all I remember the day I was told that I could not join you and my brother in the defense of our nation. I had developed a respiratory problem that prohibited me from joining you in Vietnam. It was an adventure I couldn't share with you. We always joked you had the best luck, making very near escapes both as a child and as an adult. But a day came when you cursed that luck more than any other trait you had. And when I heard the circumstances of Jack's death, I did too. In the youth of my grief I was unable to realize how fortunate I was to have only lost one brother in that fight rather than both." He paused and sucked in a huge tremulous breath, from Evan's view he could see a tear slide down his face. *The dog tags are Jack's.* Evan's face got hot and his throat began to burn. Defying impossibility, Evan's heart sank even lower, not just for himself, but for Charlie.

The old man leaned forward slightly to see his papers clearer, but as he did so he sniffed and backed away quickly, looking up as he tried to compose himself. "Forgive me, I'm trying not to see the flag." Charlie managed to choke out. Taking a few more deep breaths he began again. "You were just as much my brother as Jack was, and though I resented you at first, all was forgotten when you came back. It's been many years since we were this far apart and it seems that yet again you've gone on an adventure to a place I can't follow. You made me promise before you got cancer that I would keep an eye on your trouble making offspring, and I intend to keep it. Say hi to Jack in heaven for me. - Your Brother, Charlie." Almost breaking down completely, Charlie sat down on the bench behind the podium. Next to him was Evan's dad who stood, patted Charlie on the back and walked towards the podium. He paused and looked over the audience. Father and Son met eyes in a silent exchange of mutual feeling. As Evan met his dad's eyes he noticed just how much he resembled him, with light brown hair and two coppery brown eyes.

"Thank you all for coming. Julie wanted me to express how grateful she is that you were able to attend. After the pallbearers go out we ask that you wait until all family members have left before heading to the gravesite. Thank you." He finished and walked towards the casket gesturing for the rest of the pallbearers to join him. Evan took a deep breath before standing up and joining his dad along with the rest of the friends and relatives who had been asked to carry his grandfather to the car that would take him to his final resting place. Evan grabbed the handle and together the men lifted the casket and carried it down the aisle. Evan's muscles groaned, the casket was heavy, and the handle was cold to the touch. It was as if the weight of the casket was equivalent to all the pain and grief that had been building ever since that fateful day at the hospital. And it pressed heavily on his shoulder.

His chest ached from holding back tears, but he couldn't hold them back anymore, so silently, he let them fall. The carpet stretched before him, every step felt like it took an eternity. Finally they made it out the door and walked toward the hearse. Gravel crunched beneath Evan's feet and a cool breeze whipped around him, his hair ruffled and stuck to his tear stained face. Gently they set the casket down into the hearse. Before he let go of the handle, Evan whispered, "Bye Grandpa." Choking, Evan turned towards the church and somberly, with his dad beside him, walked back. In the church, food had been set out on tables in a back room.

"You should eat something," his dad urged, nudging him toward the table. Numbly Evan nodded his head and proceeded to fill his plate with food. Sitting down in one of the chairs he began to eat. He knew in reality the food was delicious, but nothing about this day felt real, and the food tasted like ash on his tongue. A few minutes later they were leaving for the gravesite.

Somehow Evan managed to get through all the "I'm so sorry for your losses" and the "Let me know if you need anythings" that came with funerals without crying, and headed to the car with his mother, father, and sister in tow. When they got in the car, silence reigned and not even Noel made a sound. The thin cloud cover began to disappear and the sun shone brighter than ever, mocking the somber occasion with its joyful rays.

Eventually Noel could stay silent no longer.

"Evan," she said innocently.

"Yeah?" Evan questioned, buckling himself as the car began to move.

"Why is everybody so sad today?"

"Umm, b-because.. Grandpa is going away for a long time." Evan's voice wavered and his vision blurred before him.

"Where to?" Noel inquired, but Evan couldn't answer.

"Ask Daddy," was all he managed to get out. The previous silence broken, his mom turned on an old CD of hymns that they had owned for as long as Evan remembered. Much to Evan's dismay, "Poor Wayfaring Stranger" began to play and Noel began to sing, her pure voice echoing.

"I'm just a poor wayfaring stranger, a travelin through this world of woe, yet there's no sickness toil or danger, in that bright world to which I go..." On the song went, it's haunting sound accentuated by the innocence of a child's voice. Although he was dreading having to watch his grandfather's casket lowered into the ground, he was glad when the car ride ended and he could escape, what he imagined, was the sound of death.

Finally the car stopped at a church. It was small with a tiny but beautifully maintained graveyard. They had parked next to the tent where the casket had already been unloaded and placed above the grave it would be placed in. Evan's head ached from crying and as he made his way to the tent he wished the day would end. It felt like someone was putting a sledgehammer to his eyes and he wanted it to stop. Quietly he sat down in the row of chairs. He opened his eyes staring at the casket. It was still covered in the flag and he groaned slightly when he realized what was yet to come. When the two honor guards appeared, it sealed his dread. Slowly the guests began to arrive and before he knew it the next phase of the funeral began.

Evan trembled as the honor guard began to fold the flag into triangles; once they had finished, one stepped forward and kneeled before Evan's mom.

"On behalf of the President of the United States, the United States Coast Guard, and a grateful Nation, please accept this flag as a symbol of our appreciation for your loved one's honorable and faithful service." Trembling with sobs, Evan's mom took the flag and held her palm open as he dropped three bullets into them. As they fell, Evan began to cry yet again as he remembered when his grandfather had explained to him the meaning.

Three volleys fired and three words: duty, honor, and country. Evan didn't think he could cry anymore tears, then the final blow of emotion came. The preacher came forward and spoke.

"This concludes the memorial of James Robert Coreman. We will close with taps." Then, piercing the quiet was the sound of a bugle, the notes sliced through the air and it sent chills down Evan's spine. His heart sank further. It was a song used at the closing of day, and for the closing of life. He was too overtaken with emotion to make any noise but his body shook and his lungs and throat began to ache, he gasped for air and it stung his throat. He turned to his mom who was just as indisposed; she turned and hugged him, the flag cradled between them. At last it was over, but the emotion was not. Pulling away, his mom began attaching the bullets to something. Finished, she held the item out to him.

"The chain is from his dog tags," she explained.

Evan clutched the chain, running a finger over its rough, beady surface. He could see it hanging around his grandad's neck as he smiled down at Evan, his eyes full of love for his grandson. *I'll never see him smiling down at me like that ever again.* Suddenly, the desire to be away from everyone that had shadowed him all morning was overwhelming. It constricted his chest and neck with such pain he felt he might choke. Fighting to keep his composure, he looked up and gave his mom a watery smile before saying, "I'm going to the restroom," and bolting towards the church before he started crying again. When he reached the restroom, he looked in the mirror. His face was red and blotchy with tear stains, snot was dribbling from his nose, and around his neck was his bullet necklace. *Honor, Duty, and Country* he thought, fingering them. Leaning against the granite countertop, he took several deep breaths, mastering himself once more. He turned to leave the bathroom, but gave himself one last glance that made him stop in his tracks. Looking back at him, was a pair of mismatched eyes, one brown and one bright green.

Chapter Two

Shafts of golden morning light shone through the tall windows lining the hallway, casting a cheerful glow and dancing blindingly in the eyes of the girl striding along the corridor. Squinting against the light and shifting the tray in her arms, she walked swiftly toward the door at the end of the hall. As she reached it, she carefully pulled one of her arms from beneath the tray and knocked. "Your majesty? It's Allana. May I come in?"

"Of course," a soft, calm voice answered.

Pushing open the carved door, Allana glanced into the room. Poised in front of a large mirror sat a young woman, tugging lightly on a strand of pinkish-silver hair that had come loose from her bun. Her magnificent dress spilled off the stool she sat on, its many colors glittering. Though they weren't recognizable due to being tucked neatly against the back of her clothing, what Allana knew to be a pair of glistening, butterfly-like wings fluttered slightly as they draped down, nearly touching the ground.

As Allana approached, the familiar warm, humming feeling that accompanied the unrivaled power of the May Queen settled over her. She rested the tray on the table beside her. "Do you need help preparing, your Majesty?"

"I've told you before, Allana, please call me Rosela. You know I hate having a friend call me 'your majesty'," said the May Queen, glancing over her shoulder with a warm smile. "And thank you for offering." She turned back to the mirror, continuing to squint at herself in its depths. "I've been messing with my silly hair and gown for hours now. I think it's time I just leave it be." Sitting back and relaxing, she breathed out a sigh. Her tired eyes rested on the tray of food and suddenly lit up. "Oh, thank goodness!" she said, reaching for a roll. "I haven't eaten at all today." She took a rather large bite of the bread.

"I can't imagine the look on Advisor Hyacinth's face if he saw you do that," said Allana, grinning.

"What Hyacinth doesn't know can't hurt him," muttered Rosela with a chuckle, her mouth still full of food.

Allana laughed, pulling a loose strand of purple hair away from her eyes. *This is why she's such a great May Queen; she isn't constantly fussing about what others think of her, like the other snotty court members.* Ever since she'd begun her work at the palace, she'd had the privilege of being a close friend to the queen, and was incredibly grateful for the ancient ruler's wise words and kind disposition.

The Queen's voice cut through her reflections. "So how has your morning been? Busy, I expect, with the preparations for the Ascension Anniversary."

"Oh, yes," replied Allana, stifling a yawn. "We've all been up since before sunrise, making the last touches and such. They were in such a rush in the kitchen that they even had your personal maids helping out. Of course, when I showed up, they told me they 'had all the hands they needed'. I guess they're still a little annoyed about the cake incident," she added, holding back a grin.

The Queen chuckled, brushing a crumb off of her front. "To be entirely fair, you did freeze the entire batch of batter."

"It was an accident though!" Allana said defensively, vividly remembering the look of intense exasperation and outrage on the head cook's face as she stared from the solid batter to the cowering and apologetic Allana. "That's the most worked up I've ever seen advisor Evergreen, which is seriously saying something."

Queen Rosela rolled her eyes. "Sometimes the way he overacts makes it seem like the kingdom is in a perpetual crisis. However, he does handle any leadership duties I give him well."

"I wish he would stop glaring at me every time he sees me, though," grumbled Allana. "It only happened because I was still getting used to my power after — " she quickly cut herself off to suppress the bitter memories taunting her.

Shaking herself out of her reverie, she glanced up to see Rosela staring sadly at her. Despite appearing so young, her eyes were worn with the history and wisdom of long forgotten years. They bore into Allana and made her wish she'd never brought up her past. "Allana," she said, shifting her position on the stool so that she was facing the young Fae. "They're not as different from us as everyone thinks and I know you know that. You don't need to be ashamed of who raised you."

Allana didn't respond. She couldn't really understand, she concluded bitterly. *She couldn't know how much I've had to deal with from every Fae I meet because of my upbringing.* Though she continued to glare at her clasped hands, she could tell the Queen was staring at her, wanting to say more. She opened her mouth to speak but a knock at the door cut her off.

"Your majesty?" a quiet voice from the other side of the door called.

The Queen cast one last concerned look at Allana before answering, "Come in."

The round face and dark blue eyes of Ember peered around the door. "I'm so sorry to disturb, your Majesty," she said quickly, giving a little bow, "I simply wanted to check and make sure you didn't need anything."

"Thank you for checking, Ember, but I've got all of the help I need," said the Queen kindly. "I expect they're nearly ready, then?"

"Yes, your majesty," said the queen's maid, with a little nod.

"Alright. Tell them I will be down in a moment."

"Of course," said Ember, swiftly exiting with the gentle click of the great, carved door. The May Queen stood, smoothing the front of her gown. "I guess I'd better finish up and head down there," she murmured.

As she stood, Rosela turned to Allana once more. Allana could tell by her worried eyes that she wanted to pursue the topic further, but Allana met her gaze, silently trying to tell her that she didn't wish to discuss the issue more than necessary. Finally, the Queen conceded. "Allana, will you go get my crown?" Nodding, Allana swiftly departed into the next room.

Blinking as light from the stained-glass windows struck her eyes, she gazed about for the crown. The Queen's pet stag, Solstice, watched her search with a passive expression from where he lay upon his bed of blankets, his large ears flicking about lazily. A flash of something well-polished momentarily snagged her attention, but as Allana squinted through the dazzling sunlight she could see it wasn't the crown. A long, thin sword of bright gold with a cheerful, flower- covered hilt sat upon a shelf above the stag, its immaculate patterns and unnatural sheen drawing the eye. *Oh, I was wondering where she'd moved it.* She paused to admire the sword, memories of the May Queen telling her about how exactly she made it surfacing in her mind. *It must be remarkable, having the ability to craft such a weapon with nothing but your power.* Pulling herself from her momentary reverie with a small shake, she resumed her search.

As her gaze roved over the sunlit room, another glint of bright silver caught her eye. The ancient silver crown of the

May Queen sat glistening upon its velvet red pillow, shimmering beautifully despite its incredible age. As Allana picked it up, she couldn't help but stop and marvel at it. Like the Queen's sword, the beautifully molded silver had intrigued her ever since she'd begun her work as a Queen's maid. The ornately designed flower petals, snowflakes and leaves that lined the crown had a certain unspoken magic about them, as though eons of sitting on the heads of the most powerful Fae who ever lived had imbued them with some mystical power.

Tracing a pale finger over the crown's rim, a question struck Allana that she'd never thought to ask. Turning, she headed back into the room where the Queen was still preparing herself. As she set the pillow bearing the crown next to her, she couldn't help pose her question. "Your m-Rosela," she quickly corrected herself with an apologetic grin, seeing the Fae glance over her shoulder with an expression of amusement and feigned crossness. "I'm sorry if this sounds rude, I'm just curious, but how long have you been May Queen?"

The Queen sat back from her task of pinning flowers in her hair, a thoughtful expression on her face. "I honestly forget the exact number," she finally answered. "It feels like an eternity since I was chosen. Well, it basically has been. I suppose they'll mention it during the celebration." She scooped up one of the Journey's End lilies lying in a shallow bowl of flowers, pausing to gaze introspectively upon its delicately freckled pink and white petals before gingerly sticking the flower in Allana's hair. "I know you find the Spring Court distasteful, but your hair does complement some of their decorative flowers well," she commented.

Allana smiled. "Don't let Thea hear you say that, she's been trying to convince me to let her braid flowers into my hair for weeks."

Rosela laughed, reaching for her silvery crown as Allana hopped up to grab her other belongings.

As she meandered over to pick up the Queen's cloak from where it was draped off of a nearby chair, another question occurred to her. "You mentioned that you were 'chosen' to be May Queen. I've heard Court Fae say that the power itself chooses who will be the next May Queen and when, regardless of status. But, if it doesn't care about how powerful a Fae is, how does it decide who to choose?"

Rosela, taking the cloak from Allana, gazed at it with a look on her face that suggested that she was mulling over her words carefully. Finally, she responded. "Allana,many are given power but not all know how to use it. It takes specific virtues, virtues that are sought out when looking for the next May Queen."

Allana stood in silence, mulling over the Fae's words. As she did, the Queen opened her great wings, stretching them out to their full size. The light drifting in through the windows shone through their translucent colorful membranes, bathing the area around her in colored light reminiscent of the illusion created by the stained-glass windows. She gave them a gentle flutter that sent a breeze across Allana's face. "There, ready," she murmured. "Why don't you head down to the celebration, Allana? You've been very helpful all morning, and I think I can manage getting Solstice on my own. Tell them I will be there momentarily."

"Alright." She headed for the door and slipped out, nearly bumping into the chest of a scowling Winter Court Fae, who'd clearly just been about to knock.

The tall Winter Court Fae looked down upon her as though he were staring at a crushed beetle. "There you are," his articulate voice oozed with annoyance. "Come with me. Goodness knows we could've used you thirty minutes ago. The one time you could be useful and you're not there. Figures."

Wow, and for just a moment there I thought you weren't going to say something condescending to me. How silly of me to think you have some sort of a heart, Allana thought bitterly, dying to say her thoughts out loud. Instead, she contented herself with glaring at the floor as though it had done her some deep, personal wrong. "What, is it you needed me for, sir?"

"Cian's just about having a heart attack about the fact that Gwyneth's stupid Lynx kitten has been wreaking havoc all morning, and I was told you'd be the best one to subdue the little furball." He sneered, glancing down his nearly white nose at her as they strode around a corner. "Makes sense, seeing as you're almost an animal yourself, being raised by those foul creatures."

One of these days I'm going to freeze his pointy nose right off his face, Allana vowed, clenching her fists with such ferocity that she could feel tiny bits of frost accumulating in her palms. Even before the cake incident, Evergreen had treated her as though she was something he simply had to deal with on the Queen's orders. However, the vengeful thought was suddenly wiped from her mind as an abrupt noise met her ears.

A horrible, bloodcurdling screech echoed down the hallway. The two Fae, all nastiness forgotten, stood rooted to the spot. "What was th—" Evergreen began in an appalled voice, but Allana didn't wait to hear the rest. That had been Ember, she knew it. *What's happened to her?* She burst into a sprint, dashing down the hallway as fast as her legs could carry her. Skidding around a carpeted corner, she could hear the distinct sounds of fearful sobbing reverberating toward her. *Has someone attacked her? Has she hurt herself?*

A sudden whoosh of wings over her head told her that Evergreen had caught up with her. He soared down the hallway and turned around a corner in a sharp arc. *Wait, this is the way back to the Queen's quarters. Something's happened to Ember in —* Suddenly, all of the terrifying pieces of the puzzle seemed to come together into one horrible conclusion, and Allana sprinted faster than she ever had before, toward the source of the noise. Rounding the corner, she could see the May Queen's door ajar, and hear a volley of panicked voices and cries. Solstice was bounding through the hallway, his tail held high in a banner of fear. Dodging the frantic deer and rushing up to the door, she darted inside. "What's hap—" she began, but the sight before her stopped the words in her mouth from ever coming.

Surrounded by a weeping Ember and the other Queen's maids, with Evergreen kneeling near her head, lay the May Queen, partially on her side, her great wings falling still and limp beside her. Her eyes were peacefully closed, as though she'd merely slipped into a doze.

Confusion, and icy feelings of dread made Allana's heart grow numb as she stumbled forward and dropped to her knees beside her friend. Desperately, she turned up to Evergreen. "What's wrong with her?"

Evergreen didn't respond. His already pale face was colorless and his eyes were wide in shock as he peered down at the May Queen's still face.

"*Evergreen!*" hissed Allana, fighting to keep some semblance of steadiness to her terrified voice. "What's wrong with her? We need to get her help—"

"You're such a fool!" snapped Evergreen, fear and agony tinging his retort. "Can't you see? She's dead." His voice quavered slightly as he spoke.

Allana froze, stunned, unable to breathe. The words pounded viciously in her head, yet they wouldn't sink in. All she could do was numbly stare at the body of what had once been the closest friend she'd ever had. As her eyes bore into the May Queen, she caught a glimpse of scarlet that brought her confusion roaring back up to the surface. A small, thin cut near her neck leaked blood. Though somewhat deep, it looked in no way lethal. *There's no way anybody could die from a wound that would only warrant maybe a few stitches.* "No, there's no way," she said aloud. "Nobody dies from a little cut like that. You must have made some mistake! She can't be gone." Her hollow voice trailed away as she gazed down at the fallen Fae. Even as she feebly tried to convince herself that the nightmare she was living wasn't true, she knew it was no use. Her questions about the strange little cut and who had done it vanished under the weight of the crushing numbness that swamped her.

Through the fog of grief , she heard Evergreen turn to speak to one of the maids. "Warn the palace of what's happened," he said, his voice shaking. "Her killer could still be somewhere here."

As the maid rushed out and Evergreen stood to search the room, Allana could hear the fearful cries of the maid echo through the castle. "The May Queen is dead!"

* * * * *

"The May Queen is dead!" The terrified shriek rang out from within the main room of the Queen's chambers, resounding through the surrounding area and into the ears of a cloaked figure who had ducked into the Queen's sunroom. Panting, he slipped along as quietly as he could, crouching behind one of the great flowering plants to catch his breath. As he rested there, he heard the desperate, frightened call of the Court Fae mirrored over and over, passed from tongue to tongue. However, the Fae's fearful cry caused him anything but sorrow. *Finally, it's done,* he reflected triumphantly. *The May Queen is no more. This should give me the time I need.* Still breathing heavily from the struggle, he glanced down at the short bloodstained sword gripped tightly between his ash-colored fingers. The Sword of Nulada's black surface glinted with a peculiar menace. The sheen of the blade was the only hint at its lethal nature. He knew it to be a blade that guaranteed the death of those it wounded, no matter how minor the injury. *It has served me well in clearing the way to my goal.* He couldn't help but smirk in spite of himself at the memory of the May Queen's shock. She'd been powerless to stop the sword and the quick death it brought with it. *Who would have thought some old heirloom of my father's would be what brought the great May Queen to her knees,* he relished. Ever so carefully, he wiped the weapon off on his dark cloak, knowing very well that the slightest flinch could end his life.

Suddenly, he could hear voices nearby. Hushed, frightened, and angry voices. They were searching for him. Standing up from his resting spot, he slunk over to the doors leading out onto the balcony and eased them open. He strode out unto the elegant marble surface, feeling the cool morning air blow across his face. The day was steadily turning dreary as gloomy clouds had begun to form, obscuring the shafts of light that had been streaming through unto the kingdom below. Leaping up onto the marble rampart, the cloaked Fae paused to survey what was before him. The grand, mystical land of Aeternum stretched as far as his eyes could reach, even from the top of the great Court Palace. *Soon,* he thought with a twinge of excitement. *Soon this land will be under my control.* As the voices of the searching Fae grew closer and closer, he opened his wings, massive, jet- black wings that cast the area around him into shadow.

Smirking, he let himself fall from the balcony, vanishing like a shadowy apparition into the trees below.

Chapter Three

As the parakeets tweeted and the guinea pigs ran around in their cages, Evan grabbed the receipt. "Here you are, ma'am." He handed the grey-haired lady the receipt with her bag full of cat treats. He watched her gather up her things, wondering why she felt the need to have the amount of cats required to consume that many treats. She thanked him and smiled before hobbling out of the pet shop. Sighing happily, he closed the cash register and stretched. He was finally done with his long shift for the day. Although he loved his job, it was still stressful running it by himself. *I'm still kind of surprised the manager lets me run the store by myself.* She said that she felt like Evan had a special connection and really knew how to take care of animals. She wasn't wrong. He really did love animals. He flipped the sign on the front door that said OPEN to CLOSED.

As he was walking around the store saying goodbye to each and every pet, like usual, he grabbed his bag and pulled it over his shoulder. Milling around each aisle, he carefully checked that each animal had food and water. Parakeets and budgies chirped cheerfully at him as he passed, and he paused to give one of the rats a loving scratch as the little rodent scampered up to the glass to greet him. Chuckling under his breath, he shut off the lights in the backroom and started towards the front door. As he grabbed the handle of the rusty entrance, he searched the pockets of his jeans for the key to lock up. When he finally found it, he locked the door and tugged it to make sure it was secure. After walking about three feet away from the entrance, it occurred to him that he hadn't felt his phone when he'd searched his pockets for the store keys. *Of course I left it on the counter, if I leave it one more time I'll probably break a world record.* He rolled his eyes at himself before turning around. While fumbling with the slightly rusty lock, he noticed his neighbor standing outside. *How does he have time to randomly appear like this?*

"Oh, hey, Elmer," Evan said, pausing his wrestling match with the stubborn lock.

"Greetings, Evan Hale. And that's Mr. Gristle to you, young man."

He uses everybody's full names when he talks to them. I'm pretty sure he's the only person I know who does that. "Oh, sorry, sir," Evan said.

"Ugh," Elmer said in disgust, "why do you always close the shop five minutes too early? I need food for Penelope."

Ugh. Great, he brought his tarantula.

"Sorry Elmer, but I believe I'm closing on the right time. See?" He pointed to the sign where it said what time the shop closed and opened every day, double checking in the process that he was right. Fortunately, the shop schedule spelled in bold blue letters the time he had in mind, and he stifled a sigh of relief.

Elmer scoffed and said, "Very well then. I might have to put in a request to your manager about closing later than usual. Goodbye, Evan Hale." He turned sharply on his heel and passionately strolled away with his tarantula on a leash.

I love all things animals, but this guy kind of takes it to a new level. I wonder why he loves that tarantula so much, and where he got a harness small enough to fit it, Evan thought, grabbing his key and unlocking the door.

After jamming the key in the lock and yanking the hatch open, he finally entered the shop. Evan noticed something moving out of the corner of his eye. Outside the glass window stood a white eyed, purple haired, curious-looking girl. White eyes? They have to be contacts. The peculiar girl seemed to be just observing him. He quickly went and found his phone but when he looked back to see if she was still standing there, she had disappeared. He locked it

for the second time and dashed out the door. He went around
to the bush where the girl had stood, hoping she would still be
there. After a few minutes of looking for her, he gave up.

Why is she watching me? He felt a nagging sensation,
like he might've seen this girl before, but he didn't feel like
that could have been possible. Who knows, maybe she's some
stalker emo girl. He laughed at the thought, then went around
again to the front and started toward his house. Walking, he
thought to himself. It's really nice that the shop is so close to
my house.

On the way, he saw birds, to which he tossed the bird
seed that he always carried in his bag. As he hiked across a
tranquil bridge over a quiet stream, he also saw a turtle that
he always saw on the way back from the pet shop. "Hi
Georgia!" he called down to the creature, who poked her
snout higher out of the water to get a better view of him. He
fed her some turtle pellets from his bag. She happily gobbled
them up and looked up to Evan on the bridge, clearly wanting
more. He tossed the rest of the crumbs to her and kept
walking. He basically had every type of animal food stored in
his bag for occasions like this. Standing up and emptying the
remaining crumbs back into the bag, he headed in the
direction of the park he often visited, while the breezy
summer air hit his back. Something about summer made Evan
feel content. Was it the beautiful sky or maybe the way the
breeze blew through his hair? Or maybe it was the fact that all
the animals came out to greet him. As he was walking, he
brushed his brown hair away from his green eye. He found
himself thinking about the strange encounter he had with that
girl, if you could call it an encounter at all. I wonder if she was
thinking about breaking into the store or something. No,
there's no way, if she were scouting out the place she'd have
been more casual and relaxed. Plus, who breaks into a pet
shop? I guess I shouldn't overthink it, she might have just
been picking something up or something like that. Tugging

his thoughts away from the strange girl, he took a deep breath of the warm air and meandered on.

During the time that Evan came closer and closer to the park, he grabbed his lunch bag and opened it. A ham sandwich, an apple, some popcorn, and a juice box. Nice. Thanks, mom. He came across his usual bench sitting down and breathing in slowly. There was something about the air that was different in the summer. The sun was hot on his skin as he reached in the paper bag to grab his sandwich. He pulled the wrapper off the sandwich and took his first bite out of it. While he was eating, he looked around, reflecting on how any other person may not notice the interesting bustle of life in the park. He saw a tiny squirrel crawl up a tree and chuckled a bit to himself. What a cute little guy. He glanced up at the small sea of beautiful wildflowers littering the sunny ground before him. Maybe I could pick some for Noel, she would like that, Evan thought to himself.

Watching a duck and her ducklings waddle around the edge of the nearby pond, he grabbed his phone and plugged in his earphones. He turned it on and shuffled his playlist. To his dismay, a song that his grandfather loved came on. A pang shot through his chest. It reminded Evan of him. He didn't know how to feel, listening to it again. Emotion washed over Evan, a bittersweet feeling that for some reason comforted him, as though he was still holding a small piece of his grandfather. He grabbed the juice box. He did love anything peach flavored. His mother usually packed his lunch and she knew how much he loved peaches or anything containing them. Taking another sip he resisted swallowing and simply let the substance sit on his tongue. Ha, my mom knows me too well. He got up from the bench and started for the flower filled field in front of him. He bent down and picked up a purple flower. It reminded him of the vibrant purple hair of the girl that had been staring through the window. He picked a few more flowers and then went back to sit down. Smelling the flowers, he set them down by his bag on the bench beside him neatly. Settling himself back on the wooden bench, he stuffed his hand back inside his lunch bag.

As the heat beat down on Evan's face, he breathed in the last few minutes of enjoyment at the park. *I guess it's time to go.* He got up and took a few steps before he noticed something behind the trees. A huge, shaggy black head with a warm brown muzzle poked from the foliage with a welcoming grunt. "Oh! Vincent," Evan said, running towards the ginormous, furry black bear. He stopped right by Vincent to pet him and then remembered he had extra popcorn. He murmured to himself while getting it from his bag.

"Of all the things for a great bear like you to enjoy, popcorn certainly isn't what comes to mind. "As a smile spread across Evan's face, he pulled out the bag of popcorn his mom had packed him earlier in the day. As he opened the bag, Vincent huffed with excitement. Evan held out a handful of popcorn. The bear ate it so fast with his huge teeth that Evan worried the bear might accidentally snatch up his fingers with it. "Slow down buddy! You're going to take my hand off!" After he gave Vincent all of the popcorn, he reached over again to scratch the bear's shaggy neck. *Okay, I can spend just a little more time here and then I'll go home.*

Evan stroked Vincent's nose gently. Even though Vincent was only a bear, Evan still talked to him like a human being. Evan loved Vincent's wonderful companionship. It looked to him like Vincent felt the same way. He continued petting Vincent, talking to him cheerfully. "Vincent, I missed you a lot. You never come say hi to me anymore," Evan said, pushing back his hair.

In his head, a deep, calming voice replied with *well, I'm sorry. I'm just scared of humans. You're the only one I truly like.* Evan found himself always making up voices when talking to animals. "Well—" Evan said but then glanced up for a second and saw someone with purple hair, coming closer and closer. *No way!* Could it have been the girl he saw today behind the glass window at the pet shop? Probably not. Even as he thought it, he looked up just to make sure. The girl he saw was standing a little ways away from him. He could see even from the distance between him that the girl's face looked anything but friendly.

* * * * *

Allana froze, the boy had spotted her. She had been trailing him since the pet shop, and had been ready to accept the fact that she had been wrong. Until a giant bear walked placidly out of the woods and gratefully ate the boy's popcorn. *Normal people don't pet wild black bears.* She was still in shock, watching him. *He's the one, for sure. I'll have to be really careful about this. If he really is the one, then he could be a serious threat to me. Should I be approaching him on my own? Should I go back and find backup? It's too late, he's already spotted me.* She bit back the stab of apprehension, shaking her head. *No, I was appointed for this. I need to see it through. Plus, if he were to kill me now, he'd have basically blown his whole cover, right?* She needed to get closer. She took a deep breath and walked forward.

Chapter Four

Evan watched in bewilderment as the girl strode the last few steps across the flowery field toward him, her face set. She stalked up to him and glared with a strange, knowing look made all the more intimidating by her ghostly white irises. "Just what do you think you're doing?"

"What?" stuttered Evan, perplexed. "What do you—"

"Oh, don't play dumb when the entire Fae population is trying to track your power," growled the girl. "I know who you are." She crossed her arms and glowered down at Evan. She was a good few inches taller than him, which didn't help with his nervousness.

"You— wait, what?" asked Evan, now more confused than ever. "Er, I'm sorry, but I think you have me confused with someone else, and isn't a Fae like some sort of mythical creature?"

"Seriously?" queried the girl, her voice oozing with exasperation. "How can you even try to pretend you aren't a Fae while that bear is standing right next to you."

"Oh, Vincent." Evan felt warm popcorn- scented breath against his arm. He glanced over his shoulder to see the beast giving the purple- haired girl what almost looked like a reproachful glare. *I don't like this one, she's awfully rude,* the voice in his head murmured. He reached out and gently patted the bear's thick neck. "Yeah, I guess he's pretty chill for a black bear. Maybe he was raised by people or something like that." In the beginning he'd also wondered why the bear was so friendly, but Vincent had shown up several months ago, right after his grandfather's passing, when he really needed a friend, so he hadn't questioned it much.

Shaking himself out of his reverie, Evan glanced up to see the girl stroke the bear with an incredulous and confused expression. "Vincent," she said, staring at the bear's scar- laden, beach ball sized head. "You named the giant, battle-worn bear *Vincent*. And how can you even deny that that's weird, he's literally talking to you!"

"Why not?" stammered Evan in response, slightly defensively. "It's a cool name. And I'm not sure what you're talking about. He's an animal, how is he supposed to talk?" *Can she hear the weird voice?* The odd thought entered Evan's head, heightening his suspicion, but he ignored it. *No, that's ridiculous… right?* The girl continued to scowl at Evan, her pale eyes scrunched in annoyance and disbelief. "Er, I like your contacts," said Evan, searching for something kind to say to lighten the conversation. "They're really cool."

If the girl hadn't been scowling before, she certainly was now. "*These aren't contacts.*"

"Oh," mumbled Evan, feeling his face grow slightly warm. Unable to think of any way to respond, he stood in uncomfortable silence. He heard Vincent huff as he squelched across a patch of muddy ground from last night's rain, heading off toward the woods. *I'll see you later, Evan. You seem like you have this under control.* Evan found himself silently begging the bear to stay before remembering that the bear couldn't really talk, much less have a telepathic bond with him. *At least, I think he can't…*

The girl seemed strangely thrown off; her irritability had lapsed into a confused and ponderous silence. Finally, after an awkward, drawn-out moment, she sighed. "Look, you don't seem to be who I thought you were, so let's just start over. You have no idea what Aeternum is?"

As she spoke, the girl pulled a strand of purple hair that had fallen in front of her eyes and tucked it behind a strangely pointy ear. Evan stared at it, then glanced at her eyes, finding himself wondering if her hair was dyed or not.

Pulling himself out of his confused pondering, he tried to focus on her question. "Aeter-what? Is that a place? Or another word for Fairy like you were mentioning earlier, you know the little flying creatures."

"Little flying…? N-no, it's a place," responded the girl, seeming confused at his response. "Come on, surely you have at least heard the word. It's really similar to the word *eternal* in one of your human languages. Latin, correct?"

"Sorry, I've never heard of it." Evan felt slightly distracted as he responded. Now that the conversation had become less intense, he was aware of an odd feeling. It was neither hot nor cold, but it was somehow reminiscent of warmth, like walking outside into the perfect day. He tore his attention away from it; there were much stranger things at hand. "Why are you asking me about all of this?"

The girl sighed, brushing her hair away from her eyes again. "If you are who I think you are, explaining this will be wasting valuable time. I'll tell you more about my world later, once you prove yourself to be as benign as you're acting."

Her world? Aeternum? Latin?! It all sounded like a bunch of nonsense, and that this stranger was pulling his leg, but her odd appearance and the strange sensation radiating off of her seemed to say otherwise. He shook his head, feeling like this was all some strange dream, something spawning from one of the adventure-filled stories his grandfather had often told him. "Ok, but what does that have to do with me?"

The girl glanced over her shoulder before turning back to Evan; she seemed oddly antsy. "Well, recently, our queen was assassinated by someone whose power was detected to be from the Shadow Court— "

"The who? Someone was murdered? You need to call the police," interrupted Evan in worried confusion, but the girl ignored him. She seemed almost lost in thought as she spoke.

"Everyone believes it's the former Shadow Court king, Tablarye, who's been missing for years now. Half the Fae kingdom has been trying to track his power, including me. That's why I'm here." She looked up at Evan, her suspicious, squinted gaze returning. "I tracked the power to you."

"W-what?" exclaimed Evan, shock and disbelief flooding through him. This all seemed so ridiculous and strange. "But how? Why?"

"I don't know," admitted the girl, glancing around again. "But what I do know is that if any other court member gets ahold of you, you're dead. You have to come with me."

Evan stared at her, nonplussed, unable to respond. *This is insane,* he thought. His brain was spinning with everything she'd told him, and he felt unable to make sense of any of it. *It all just seems like a weird elaborate prank.* Finally, he looked up. "I'm sorry if this sounds rude, but how do I know you're telling the truth, and this isn't just some trick?"

The purple haired girl stared back at him, looking anxious and annoyed. She glanced over her shoulder one final time before answering. "Well, something tells me that your eye hasn't always been green. Is that true?" Her tone was almost reminiscent of an irritated school teacher explaining a concept to a confused child that they'd already been forced to repeat over and over.

Evan stared in astonishment, managing a slight nod. "Y- yeah," he stammered. "It changed a few months ago, right after my grandpa passed." The bitter flood of memories of tearful nights and grief was stifled by his mounting shock. *Nobody could ever figure out why it changed color.*

"That's what I thought," the girl responded. "Green is typically the color of Shadow Court Fae's eyes."

Evan stood still, trying to take in what this meant. *This all seemed like a practical joke before she mentioned my eye. I mean, how can I explain away something that I don't even understand?* Before he could properly get his thoughts in order to respond, he saw movement over the girl's shoulder. What was obviously the form of Mr. Gristle was poking out from around a bush, eyes wide. Instantly, Evan felt a thrill of unease. The elderly man's body was stiff and hunched over, as though he'd been trying to creep up on them. As the disquiet grew, Evan gave himself a little shake. *He's a strange old man with an obsession for his pet tarantula,* he reasoned, *this behavior really isn't that strange when you consider that. Plus, the park is really close to his yard, so maybe he's just wanting to accuse me of 'trespassing' again.* He cleared his throat and gave his strange neighbor a little wave. "Oh, er, hi Mr. Gristle! Sorry, I know you hate people milling around near your property. We'll be heading out."

Mr. Gristle froze, looking shocked. It was evident he didn't think he could be seen. The girl, who'd whipped around when he'd started speaking, was looking at the grey old man with an expression of equal shock. Gristle, staring at her with beady green eyes, stood up straighter. His gaze seemed to harden, and his brow began to furrow. Evan had the odd impression of a cat about to leap. His fear rising, Evan glanced over at the girl, wondering vaguely if the boldness she'd shown earlier when striding up to him could possibly scare the man off. However, her eyes weren't fixed on his; she was looking down at his partially hidden right hand. Slowly, Evan followed her gaze to his gnarled, ashen fingers. Clutched within his skeletal grasp was unmistakably a brilliant silver dagger, glinting in the shafts of sunlight.

Instantly, Evan felt a rush of terror, and his heart began to flutter like a trapped bird. He saw the purple- haired girl step closer to him, and Gristle made his move. A blast of jet- black cloudy material swamped the man, so dark that he seemed to be immersed in a shadow. It swirled and billowed like a miniature thunderstorm, then began to wane slightly. Out of the cloud appeared a terrifyingly tall, cloak-clad man with piercing green eyes, his skin a deadened, grey tone and his horrifyingly sharp teeth bared in a menacing grin. "Well, I knew they'd find you sometime, Evan Hale," he hissed, his eerie emerald eyes fixed on Evan. "I suppose it's now or never."

Then, Evan saw the girl move. She drove her foot into the nearby mud puddle, sending a shower of droplets into the air and toward the petrifying being that had once been his neighbor. Before Evan's eyes, the droplets seemed to change, plummeting down toward the shadow-swamped being like tiny knives. As they struck his skin, he pulled back and howled in pain, and Evan realized that the droplets had frozen into tiny icicles in midair. Before his mind could process any of what had just occurred, he felt the girl grab his wrist in a tight grip. "RUN!" she shouted, giving him a hard pull. Stumbling, Evan dashed to keep up. They bolted toward the towering trees marking the beginning of the forest, their shoes pounding the flower strewn grass. Evan could hear footsteps behind him and chanced a glance over his shoulder. "Gristle" was right on their heels, his teeth bared. He was gaining on them. Terrified, Evan turned and ran harder than he ever had before, desperate to keep up with the strange girl who's power seemed his only chance. Bursting into the forest, Evan leapt over a slimy log, with the girl dodging around it. A squelchy thump and a deep grunt told him their pursuer had less success jumping the fallen tree, though he didn't dare look back.

"Where are we—" shouted Evan, clumsily sidestepping a patch of brambles, but the girl cut him off.

"Just trust me!" she responded breathlessly. She glanced over her shoulder and let out a small squeak, but before Evan could turn around, he felt a claw-like hand lock unto his shoulder, digging painfully into his collar bone.

However, just as soon as the hand had grabbed him, it disappeared, and he heard a loud bellow.

Whirling around, he saw Vincent slamming Gristle down with one massive paw. While squirming and gasping beneath the enormous bear's weight, Evan could see the shadowy being summoning up the strange darkness, clearly intending to strike back. "Don't hurt him!" he shouted. He wanted to rush to help Vincent, but the fear fueled adrenaline that had kept him running before left his feet rooted on the spot. He felt a clammy hand seize his, tugging it urgently.

"Come on! The bear can handle it, we have to go!" As she gave his arm another hard tug, Evan gave Vincent an apologetic glance, swallowed his fear for his friend, and ran.

For what felt like an eternity, the two pounded onward, dodging trees and leaping ditches. With each agonizing breath he took, Evan felt like the effort might rip his lungs straight out. The cramp in his side made him feel as though he'd been stabbed with the silver dagger, and his face stung from being whipped with branches. The girl was clearly feeling the same effects; she was gasping sharply and beginning to slow down. As they slowed to a jog, Evan became aware of how deathly silent this part of the forest was. He'd never been this deep into it before, even on walks with his grandfather when he was young. *I expected it to be a little livelier, to be honest,* he thought, *it's kind of dim and intimidating.*

Suddenly, he became aware of another pair of jogging footsteps, growing louder and faster. He was opening his mouth to say something to the girl when a burst of black substance swooped across their path, creating a wall of shadow. The pair slammed on the brakes, wheezing and staring around for the source. As Evan turned, staring into the gloomy shadows of the forest, he heard a strange *whoosh* and a gasp from behind him. He whirled around to see the girl being tossed through the air as the strange wall seemed to strike her. She landed with a painful thump several feet away. Evan wheeled around to see the shadowy form of his "neighbor" striding from the fog.

"Pathetic," the creature growled, drawing the dagger. "I honestly thought even a human could put in a better effort, how disappointing. You had to cower behind a teddy bear and a little girl in order to survive even this long."

His blood pounding in his ears, Evan made a lunge for a clear space beside the shadowy entity, but felt a hand seize him immediately. A powerful arm locked around his neck, cutting off his windpipe. Gasping and struggling frantically, Evan could only watch as he raised the dagger. The blade rushed toward him, and Evan felt an odd surge, as though something inside of him was making one last effort to live. Suddenly, there was an odd blast of pure and complete darkness, and he heard Gristle yell as the feeling seemed to leap from him. Suddenly, the dagger had dropped to the ground, the hand had vanished from his neck, and he was slumped down, gasping weakly on the wet leaves of the forest floor. Glancing over his shoulder, he saw the shadowy Gristle slowly picking himself off of the ground with a groan. Staggering to his feet as quickly as his violently shaking body would allow, Evan turned to see the girl, too, standing up. For a moment, her pale eyes flicked from Evan to the fallen form of their shadowy would-be assassin, shock and realization filling them. Finally, she gave her head a little shake, and frantically beckoned Evan.

"We need to get out of here before he recovers," she said quickly.

"Recovers from what?" stammered Evan. His brain was moving at a snail's speed, as though it had stopped working in preparation for death and was only just now realizing he was still alive.

"From you!" said the girl in a half- frantic, half-annoyed voice, tugging Evan along once more.

What does that mean? Evan thought in feverish confusion. Once again breaking off into a desperate sprint, she tugged Evan deeper and deeper into the forest's mysterious depths. A lone stag paused to watch them as they rushed past, ears twitching. Evan tried to make eye contact as he dashed by, silently begging the animal to help them.

He heard the girl yell through labored breathing. "We're nearly there!"

Thank goodness, thought Evan, though the relief was short-lived. Just as the pair burst out into a clearing, Evan heard an angry snarl. "He's right behind us!" he cried in terror. The girl didn't answer. Her eyes were fixed on something at the other end of the clearing. Evan followed her line of sight to an odd ring of toadstools surrounding a shaft of sunlight streaming in through the canopy. For one moment, Evan found himself thinking of the fantasy stories he'd been told as a kid of mythical beings making their homes in the toadstools. As they rushed toward the small ring, Evan heard the pounding feet behind him grow steadily louder and louder, and could now hear every gasping breath of the assassin. His heart felt like it would burst straight out of his chest from terror and effort as they raced for the odd ring that seemed to be their only hope. Moments from his foot hitting the sunny ground within the toadstool ring, Evan chanced a glance over his shoulder. The nightmarish sight of the shadow-immersed assassin was lunging for him, mouth open in a snarl, a talon-like leaden hand wreathed in dark substance reaching out, mere inches from grasping him. Then, his foot hit the circle of light.

Instantly, there was a great flash of blinding light, and Evan felt as though he was racing through nothingness. Though no wind blasted his face and tugged at his clothes, he was racing onward, faster and faster, until he felt as though he might pass out. Suddenly, the light dimmed, the rushing feeling stopped. Evan lay there, gasping, wheezing, unable to do anything but lie there in exhaustion. Slowly, he became aware of the comforting smell of wildflowers wreathed around him, and he heard the distant droning of a bee searching for nectar. He heard the sweet calls of a nearby songbird, and felt a warm shower of sunlight across his face. Whatever this was, it most certainly wasn't the dank, dark forest he'd come from.

Chapter Five

Allana blinked as cheerful sunlight met her eyes, a far cry from the gloomy forest they'd come from. Still panting from their long sprint, she closed her eyes with a sigh of relief. *We made it. That Shadow Court operative can't use the ring. We're safe.*

As she paused to reflect gratefully on her lucky escape, Allana heard a breathless grunt from beside her. Glancing down, she saw the boy lying flat on his back, staring dazedly up at the sky as though he couldn't believe what had just happened. He turned his head to stare at Allana, looking lost and flighty. "Wh— where did Gristle go— what just happened?" He stammered weakly.

"We escaped using that ring of mushrooms. We're in Aeternum now." Picking a twig out of her hair, Allana glanced expectantly down at the human, waiting for him to get up.

The boy rolled over and shakily sat up, but didn't get to his feet. "So what exactly is Aeternum?"

Allana bit back a snippy answer. *Now that we're somewhat safe, I guess I could tell him a little.* "It's my world, the world of the Fae." She tapped her foot, hoping the blatant cue would get through to the human.

Not even glancing at her loudly tapping foot, the boy gawked up at her as though she'd said something absolutely insane.

"Can I just explain later?" snapped Allana, causing the boy to flinch. *Gosh, how clueless is he?* "I'm sure you must be able to tell by now that the situation that caused me to bring you here is urgent. Now, please get up, we can't waste anymore time." She glared in annoyance down at the human, who blinked back at her, looking rather stunned.

"Okay," he said slowly, his forehead creased with worry and confusion. "But you will eventually explain to me what's going on, right?"

"Yes, yes, of course," promised Allana, beckoning him while fighting to keep in an annoyed outburst. "Now, come on." She turned, intending to stride off.

"Wait!" called the boy. Allana halted, biting her lip and letting out a long, tense breath. She heard the rustle of him standing up. "Can you at least tell me your name?"

Allana clenched her fists, but reluctantly relented. "Allana," she said. "My name's Allana."

"That's a nice name," said the boy, trotting up to stand next to her. "My name's Evan."

Allana grunted and began walking, jerking her head in a gesture for him to follow.

"We'll head for the Summer Court castle. Athena should be able to tell whether or not this human is who we're looking for," Allana said, whispering to herself.

As she was walking with Evan, she noticed something. He looked troubled, almost scared and she wondered why. Possibly because he practically jumped into a new world he'd never experienced or seen before. She'd been scared too. But at the same time he looked as if he were very fascinated. *Why is he scared? If I have the right person he shouldn't be this... innocent. What if you have the wrong person?* She shook her head, trying to convince herself that she wouldn't care about what happened to a stupid human being. Yeah, she definitely wouldn't.

As they were walking, getting closer and closer to the Summer Court's part of the kingdom, she looked at Evan. He was always pushing his brown hair away from his eyes. He walked almost sluggish, as if he was tired. He had on blue jeans that were a bit faded and ripped right by the knees. He wore a t-shirt. Understandable. It was super hot in the summertime. *He doesn't even know he's possibly falling into a trap.* Her stomach turned. *He's a murderer in disguise, if you feel bad for him you're just falling prey to his ruse.* Her head felt hot as she pressed the back of her icy hand to it. They kept walking. *He looks so innocent, so guiltless. But that couldn't possibly be the case. He wouldn't be here if it was. Plus, I wouldn't have seen all of the small coincidences that happened with him. He isn't guiltless. He is guilty. Or someone is.* Shooing the thought from her head, Allana tried to focus on her mission. She had to find Athena . *I'll need a Skynjari Volur to sense whether or not I have the right one, and I know for a fact she's the only one who will help me.* Allana had to make sure, for the last time, that she definitely got the right person to go on trial and be executed. Even as she thought about it, it made her feel ill. She felt her head throbbing.

"I need to sit down." She plopped down on a nearby big, red, white dotted mushroom that was fit to be a chair. Evan tilted his head, probably a little confused as to where they were going and why she looked so pale. *What if I had the wrong person all along? If so, this could possibly ruin his life.* Allana let out a breath, pushed her hair out of her eyes and heaved herself off the mushroom. They had no choice but to keep going. She had no choice.

Allana stalked along at swift space, her lips pursed and her eyes set firmly ahead. Her companion was gawking at the huge mushrooms, the size of a kitchen chair, and trees that were as tall as the sky. On the trees hung strange looking fruits, and the leaves that wreathed around them were glowing a deep blue. Allana didn't pay them, or her companion, any mind. *The sooner I rid my hands of him the better.* The crunching of following feet suddenly stopped. Allana sighed and turned around, Evan was bending over a patch of snapdragons. *Idiot!* Allana leaped forward and slapped his hand away.

"Evan! Don't touch those! They bite!"

"But they look so pretty!"

"Evan, they will literally rip your hand apart." *They're snapdragons, snap is literally in the name!* Before Allana could recover from Evan's last bout of ignorance,he was at it again.

"Gah!" Evan screamed behind her. *Can't he just keep his hands to himself for ten minutes?* Allana grumbled, before turning around to see Evan gawking at a swarm of Hestflue, tiny horses with translucent wings. Slumping her shoulders, Allana contemplated weather or not to continue or give him a few minutes to interact with the Hestflue. One had landed on his shoulder and Allana could see he was trying not to scare it. Sighing she walked over, picked it up from off of his shoulder and held it.

"Here, hold it," she said while nonchalantly passing it to Evan.

He reached out for it, an expression of wonder on his face as it jumped into his hand. The horse was brown, with purple and yellow wings. He looked around, eyes wide open. The horse pranced with its ears pricked up toward him, letting out a cheerful nicker. Evan laughed and began petting it with his index finger. *Fine, I'll let him play with it for a few more minutes,* Allana thought, then continued to observe the interaction. The tiny creature leaned into the boy's finger, gingerly scratching its shoulders, its eyes blissfully closed. Evan set the horse on his shoulder and played around with it for a bit. He looked around at the flowers falling from a tree and different colorful plants sticking up from the ground,all different shapes and sizes.

A bird chirped overhead and Allana held her hands in a cup shape and a heart-shaped bird landed in them. Evan was looking at it, his eyes wide. He obviously wanted to hold one, and sure enough within seconds he let the little horse go and picked up the bird from her hands. The bird chirped and Evan smiled. More birds appeared chirping in harmony with the one in Evan's hands. Allana began to walk again, following a path through a sparse wood, and the flock of birds flapped off chirping happily.

They loped along the well worn path that wound through the glimmering wood. Allana stared at the ground, contemplating what she would be forced to do to get answers. *Athena is in the left wing of the castle and we're coming in from the right side. The servant passages should lead straight to her hallway. The opening to the passages on the right wing is next to the-* A gasp rang out from behind her. Allana her reverie broken Allana looked around. Sprawling before them was a beautiful, sandy beach, with gentle aqua waves lapping against the golden shore. Up ahead mountains soared above them and created cliffs above the endless ocean. In between these mountains lay a valley. From that valley a cacophony of sound echoed towards them.

* * * * *

Evan was in awe. Beautiful green mountains towered above him, wind blew through his mussed hair, small sand granules stinging his face. Judging from their general direction; he guessed they were headed for the large valley up ahead, the dusky light wreathing it in shadow. An awful ear shattering noise drowned out the rush of the restless ocean and Evan resisted the urge to plug his ears.

"What is that?" he called, his hands twitching closer to his ears. Allana didn't seem to notice the obnoxious sound of an echoing wind instrument.

"That. Is the Valley of Horns, one of the Summer Court capitals. We'll have to enter the castle through a side passage." Her face was sour when she mentioned the name of the valley.

"One of the capitals?" Evan asked, his feet plodding along in the sand.

"Don't ask, you'll just be more confused," Allana answered, exasperation dripping from her voice.

"Well then what's the other capital?" They had entered the valley now and the noise was almost painful. Somehow, Allana managed to sigh loud enough that Evan heard her. To his relief, she still replied.

"It's called the Isle of Drums, it's an island fifty miles into the sea, where the other half of the Summer Court population lives. And before you ask, my throat is getting tired from yelling over the horns. So you'll just have to be confused." Silence reigned between them, though the horns were still blaring. Finally, they came upon a giant stone castle built into the cliff side. Evan continued to ogle at the castle while Allana led him to the right side of the structure, trailing along the edge of the mountains. Making their way towards the right wing of the castle, Allana pressed her hands against a series of stones leaving small ice spots on each of them. Quickly, a six by two section of the wall slid open. Evan gasped yet again.

* * * * *

The passage was lit by tiny sconces lining the wall, it was rather cramped because it hadn't widened out from the size of the door. At last, Allana stopped and turned to the left. Opening a beautiful wooden door they stepped out into a brightly painted hallway.

"Here we are, Athena's rooms are the first room on the right." Quickly Allana turned and knocked on the bright white door.

In about ten seconds, a girl with long, red hair opened the door. She had goggles with blue lenses over her head and wore a knee length, Caribbean blue dress that swished and swayed as she moved. She was surprised to see Allana. Allana smiled and then said, "Athena! Hi!" Athena jumped and hugged Allana tightly. She always did this. Allana loved Athena for it.

"What brings you here?" Athena said, with a slight accent peculiar to the Summer Court. .

"I just need some help," Allana said, looking at Evan. Athena mouthed *oh* and then swinging the door wide open motioned with her hands for them to come in and make themselves at home.

They both walked into the house and sat down on red and green metal chairs. Her house was full of colors, as always. Athena was such a sweet, caring person. *People would never think Athena would have been the type of person to have gone through the things that she did at such a young age.* Athena had always been such a good friend to Allana and she was glad to have kept her friendship so long despite societal difficulties.

"Would you like some uyu juice? I just made some today!" Athena made juice out of the fruit in the castle courtyard The fruit was teal and at night the uyus glowed orange. The fruits were very popular in Aeturnum. They tasted delicious and were many people's favorite because they healed all wounds on the skin in less than four hours.

"Yes, please. Evan, would you like to try some?" She looked at Evan, waiting for his answer.

"Sure, I don't know what that is but I'll take some." Athena chuckled under her breath and got three wooden cups. She poured the uyu juice out of the pitcher and gave them each their own cup. Allana started drinking, watching Evan over the rim of hers. He was hesitant and before he started to drink, he smelled it. He then took a sip and widened his eyes. She could tell he liked it because after that, he chugged it down and asked for another cup.

"Alright, I know what this is about, but I want the details anyway," Athena prodded, sipping her uyu juice in anticipation. Allana rolled her eyes before acquiescing.

"Well, I found him near the Blightwood border, and used the ring to travel just outside glacial falls. He befriended a bear which confirmed my suspicions."

"Oh, was the bear cute? Tell me about him." Athena practically bounced in her seat. Evan opened his mouth to respond but Allana beat him to it.

"Athena I wasn't paying attention to the bear, I was paying attention to the undercover Shadow Fae that tried to thwart me."

"So they were tracking him as well?"

"He was undercover as his neighbor. I think it's safe to say he's been watching him for some time."

"Well I guess those are the important details, so we should probably get down to business."

They looked at each other and simultaneously turned towards Evan. Evan, meanwhile, had been following the conversation with as much understanding as a confused squirrel.

"Ok, Evan. So, you're here for a reason. The reason is that you might have..." she trailed off in thought, "let's just call it a power. I'm going to have to touch your hand to understand where or how you got this ability." Athena then asked for Evan's hand and he stretched it out. *Well, that's a good sign. He would have refused if he was hiding something.* He placed his hand on top of Athena's and she took her other hand and placed it around his. "Here we go, Evan." Athena then closed her eyes. Evan looked mildly confused. Allana just wanted to know if she was right. "Oh, oh good," Athena said, "you've only inherited." Allana was shocked but at the same time she was also a bit happy. *She was still right, after all. But the question was, how did he inherit the shadow heir's power and was it even the shadow hier's power? He's only a human, so it was a little weird. They just had to talk about this and figure it out. I doubt Evan knew about it.*

Realization seemed to dawn on his previously puzzled face.

"I think that's why all of these weird things have been happening to me. I didn't know it was possible to have power!" He was bouncing with excitement. *We'll see how long that lasts,* Allana thought, before delivering the information to him. "Technically, it's not possible, for a human such as you, to have a power unless someone in your family passed it on to y—"

Evan cut her off and then went on to say, "My grandfather. He passed away a few months ago a-and," his voice trembled. He still couldn't even talk about it. "At the funeral, for some reason, one of my eyes changed color. I don't know why. It just did. My grandfather was always a little bit secretive about some things that he did. Maybe there was something he didn't want me to know. Something big."

Athena nodded her head. "Uh huh. That makes sense. Well, at least we don't have to kill you!"

"Kill me?" Evan looked at Allana. She considered grinning menacingly at him, but reluctantly decided against it, and simply chuckled.

Evan shook his head in bewilderment. But Allana didn't much care how confused he was as long as she got answers.

"Other than the bear, have you had any other strange things happen to you lately?" she asked. Evan nodded emphatically, "Yeah there was this one time where I thought a dog was talking to me but I thought I just made all of these voices up for different animals. I told the dog to come to me from across the street. There was a car coming so I said stop and the dog did. He then said thank you. I thought it was all in my head but—"

Allana jumped in and said, "But it's not. How did your grandfather have this so-called 'power'?

Allana shifted her position on the chair. She grabbed the wooden cup and sipped from it while looking Evan's way. Evan lifted his head up looking directly at her. His eyes glistened from the sun shining through the window in front of them. Allana attempted to break his reverie. "Evan," Athena said, "it might be very hard to believe but you have something very special that was passed down to you. You might have wondered why you're gifted with animals. It's because you have Fae abilities that have been given into your family line by a very powerful Shadow Court member. He must have originally given them to your grandfather, and due to the nature of gifted magic, it skipped a generation and came to you when your grandfather died." Silently Allana awaited his answer.

* * * * *

Evan listened carefully. He found himself believing this. He now understood why the green eye had shown up the way it did. It made him feel a bit better. He got comfortable in the green chair and looked over at Allana. She looked around the room and then smiled. *She must have been thinking about something or remembering something.* Evan couldn't have possibly known this was for sure from his grandfather. He wasn't sure about anything at this point anymore. He was sure that everyone in the small apartment felt the same way. He still couldn't bring himself to believe that Allana was possibly trying to kill him. *Trial and execution.* Those words rang in his head like a bell.

He thought he was just a normal teenage boy up until yesterday. Even as this was all going on, he didn't think anything that exciting could have happened to him. He was just too normal to have anything like powers. He tried to make himself believe that he did have powers but for some reason couldn't. Why didn't he believe it? After everything he'd seen, he still didn't believe it. But he had to. He just had to. He shook his head and then looked at Athena.

"This juice is interesting. I've never had anything like this. "

"Yeah, mate! It's really good for wounds. It helps them heal in under four hours! Can you believe that?" Athena blew air from her nose.

Evan choked on the juice. *Only four hours? Was that even possible?* He asked Athena,

"How is that possible? I've never heard of anything like it."

She laughed. Actually the Uyu tree is quite common around here."

Evan gaped. *Definitely bringing gallons of that home with me. This is absolutely insane. It can't be real. I have to be dreaming. Maybe I fell asleep on that park bench or something. Then why are your cuts gone? This is insane.*

"Now time to get down to business, shall we, Evan?" Athena said, grabbing a piece of paper. "Please write down anything weird or out of the ordinary that has happened to you over the past few months on this paper please."

He picked up the pen and the paper and thought to himself. He started writing right away. One time he was making popcorn and he dropped a kernel on the floor. He went to pick it up and once he picked it up, it popped in his hands. The funny thing was that the kernel wasn't hot so it couldn't have just popped. He kept trying to convince himself that it was definitely hot but now thinking back, it must not have been the kernel that was super hot. It must have been his fingertips or hands, for that matter. He kept writing and after a bit, Athena stopped him.

"Okay, clearly you have some sort of power. No need to write anymore down. We know for sure now that you might be a clue to this mystery we need to solve." Athena, after saying this to Evan, looked at Allana. "Good job, Allana. After all, I did believe in you." Allana and Athena then smiled at each other.

Evan noticed it was getting dark outside. The world around

him looked magical when it became dark. Bugs lit up, different colors in the sky. So did the stars and trees. Something about this place brought Evan joy. It was beautiful. Almost like something that would be shown about a magical land on television. Yeah, it definitely was just like that.

Evan got up to stretch and asked Athena if she possibly had a bathroom anywhere around. She pointed to the end of the small room and then Evan went straight for it. As Evan was walking towards the door, he could hear the excitement in Allana's voice. She must have been excited to see Athena. They talked about things Evan didn't understand. Evan went into the small bathroom, shut the door and looked into the mirror. The mirror was slightly tilted to the left so Evan tilted it up right. Athena seemed like the person to keep everything a mess. She must have been an artistic person. He looked at himself with confidence. How amazing it felt that he had anything such as a 'magical' power. He thought to himself about how he hadn't noticed this before then shrugged. *Well, at least now I know.* He thought it was normal that people talked with animals but Allana made it very clear that it was not. He turned on the sink and left his hands under the cold running water and splashed it on his face. He looked up into the mirror once more. He really did look tired. It only made sense. A lot happened in just one day. *A lot. I wonder where Mom thinks I am. I hope she isn't too worried about me. I wish I hadn't left my phone on that park bench. Then again, I don't know if it would even work here.* The realization of how far from home he was, in a whole other universe that he didn't know existed, struck him all at once, and he swallowed hard. *I hope I can go home soon.*

Chapter Six

Allana swayed restlessly as frost sprung from her fingers and coated her hands. "Oh, warm up Allana, he may be a human but he's not that bad. Besides, aren't you curious to see his reactions to our world?" Athena admonished. Allana stopped swaying, and gave her friend a steely glance.

"He's a human. He's not supposed to be here, and it also means that we still haven't found the coward who killed the May Queen. I don't have time to babysit him." *And even if I did, why would I want to?* Her hands were white with snow and she was beginning to feel the chill in her limbs, a rare occurrence for Winter Court Fae. Athena crossed her arms and raised her eyebrow skeptically.

"Look, you can't just take him back where he came from, or the Shadow Court will get him, and even though he's human not even *he* deserves that. He also certainly can't stay here, because if any of the court finds him, especially that visiting pompous fool Hyacinth, that innocent boy will be on trial for murder before you could say percussion," Athena reasoned.

"Someone could do a lot of things within the time it takes to say percussion," Allana deadpanned.

"Very funny. The point is, if you don't want him killed by the Courts because he's a human, you need to show him around and explain some of the mechanics of our world to him, so that you might be able to pass him off as Fae, until we find the real murderer. Put him in normal clothes, take him to the Seasonless," she explained.

Allana squeezed her fists shut and the ice on her knuckles cracked. "Fine. But I'm sneaking into a Court session. I have to know who their suspects are. Any leads they have, I want to know about." She held Athena's gaze until she looked away.

"Alright, but you better clean up the ice you just got on my carpet. Honestly Allana, I told you to warm up."

"What needs to warm up?" Evan's clueless face popped out from the restroom. He walked out, brushing his hair out of his eyes. Allana raised her eyes to heaven, exasperation oozing from her as she slouched hopelessly. Athena grinned.

"Have fun on your outing," she called, giving Allana a patronizing wave.

"What outing?" Evan looked back and forth between the two Fae. Allana sighed.

"I'm showing you around Aeternum so that you will have some semblance of understanding," Allana elucidated.

"Really, when do we leave?" his eyes lit up, but the green shone brightest.

He's like a child at Christmas. I bet he's the kid that's shocked and excited about every single gift beneath the tree. That doesn't matter Allana, there is no such thing as Christmas. It's a stupid human holiday. Allana shook her head, and walked toward the door.

"You coming?" she asked, not waiting for Evan as she stalked out the door.

* * * * *

Evan panted lightly as he caught up to Allana's long purposeful strides. He wished she wouldn't walk as fast as she did, as he'd hardly had anytime to scrutinize the Summer Court castle and take in the beauty. Even beneath the blanket of darkness, the world seemed alight with magic. The stars above them seemed especially bright, filling the sky with faint yet stunning patches of blue and purple mixing with the inky black. Colorful fireflies, neon, painted the night sky. Trees with long pink branches quietly swaying in the wind. Strange, distant calls of nighttime creatures occasionally rang out from somewhere in the woods around them, unlike any animal he'd ever heard. He noticed something hopping on the ground. He looked at it and realized it was a frog. *Wait! Does that frog have black spots on it?* Instead of ribbiting, the frog mooed, which fascinated Evan. The creature was a mix of frog and cow! "So, where are we going?" he skipped to the Fae's side and matched her pace.

"I'm taking you to the Seasonless," Allana said flatly.

"Wait, the what now? Is the place just called Seasonless, or are there actually no seasons there? How can it be seasonless? Everything has a season."

"You'll see when we get there and believe me, even the Seasonless will far outshine anything remotely beautiful by human standards," Allana replied, again with the lowest amount of emotion Evan had ever heard. *Her words are haughty but her tone is so flat,* Evan thought. His confusion grew with every interaction. Evan couldn't stop smiling in awe. Not only were the Zinnias glowing, they were the largest variety he had ever seen. His mom loved to garden and Zinnia was one of her favorite flowers. Yellows, orange, pink, white, even a few blue, lit up the bushy green grass that blanketed the hillside, looking like stunning, multicolored fireflies. His hand jerked forward of its own volition, and before he knew it his arms were full of them. He looked around to see dragonflies zoom past him. Not just any dragonflies, it looked like, but these dragonflies had tiny ears on them. *Cat ears!* Behind him, a sigh passed through the air.

"If we stop for every common flower we'll be here for the next two hundred years, and I really don't want to deal with burying your fragile human body after the first century," Allana grumbled.

"Common? This level of color variety certainly isn't common, if it was, my entire yard at home would be full of them because my mother is garden gaga. Plus, I'm not sure if you noticed while you were in the human world, but our flowers don't glow." Evan looked pointedly at her. *She's a Fae. She's surrounded by flowers all the time. How does she not know this?*

"Either way, we don't have time to pick flowers. I have to make you appear somewhat normal, I want to get back into normal clothes and we have to go to the markets for that. And the market is in the Seasonless."

"Alright, I'm coming," he stuffed several of the beautiful flowers back in his pocket, hoisting the rest higher in his arms, and fought back a grin. "No need to be so frosty." The Fae's head snapped around to glare at him, looking almost astonished at how cheesy the pun was, and Evan figured he might as well continue since the damage had already been done. "What was it Athena said? Warm up, yeah. Warm up, Allana, it is the Summer Court after all!" Unable to stop himself, Evan grinned apologetically at Allana, his shoulders shaking slightly with barely suppressed laughter.

Evan held his breath. For a second he thought Allana was going to laugh. Her lips quivered and a tooth flashed from beneath them, but it was gone just as quickly as it appeared, and soon she was walking slowly down the hill after him. When she passed him, her face was downcast. A sigh escaped her lips, but she straightened and her usual look of disgust returned. Rigid, she continued on. Evan sighed to himself. He thought for a moment that he had broken through to her, and that he might have earned a friend. *It kinda seems like she wants to, though. I wonder what's stopping her from being friendlier to me. Maybe there's some sort of weird Fae rule or something?* Pity stung him slightly at the thought. Fingering his bullet necklace, he followed her.

Soon they reached a wooded area full of strong, full oaks, with branches sprawling all the way down to the ground and green light bursting serenely from the markings etched in the trunk. Despite their looming size and long limbs, the darkness of the night did anything but make them look unfriendly. Their leaning figures felt oddly inviting, and Evan longed to climb them. Resisting the urge, he turned back to Allana" Are we almost there?" he asked.

"No."

Evan was beginning to get a stitch in his side, and the flowers he was carrying were beginning to feel more like heavy tree branches than delicate blossoms. He wanted to sit and rest, maybe in one of the trees, but he sensed that any complaint would start an exchange on the weakness of humans, which would provoke him, so he stayed silent.

"Give me the flowers, they're slowing you down," Allana said and took them from his arms.

"Thank you," he nodded. The Fae scowled deeply, but snatched up the flowers nonetheless. Evan slowed down so he would be behind her so that she could not see his enormous eye roll. *I guess saying thank you is annoying too, now?* Shaking the slightly bitter thought from his head, he trudged on, contenting himself with peering around in barely contained wonder at the small groups of luminous, spotted lizards, which leapt from the glimmering trees and occasionally scampered across their path. Finally, they stopped. Allana set the flowers down and sat on the ground.

"Are we at the Seasonless?" Evan's voice was filled with hope.

"Does this seem seasonless to you?" She raised an eyebrow.

"Well, there are oak trees pretty much everywhere so..." Evan trailed off, still standing and fingering his necklace.

"We are resting before continuing, you have been lagging for the past half hour."

"We've only been walking for a half hour."

"Case in point," Allana smirked slightly before grabbing silver berries off a nearby bush and tossing them in her mouth.

Evan opened his mouth to give a pithy reply, but his brain was short on such responses and he was thus stuck standing with his mouth agape for several long moments before finally resolving to let it slide, and sit. Allana tossed him some berries. Evan turned his nose up.

"They taste like strawberries," she assured him.

"I will be able to eat other food, right? I won't have to live on the courtesy of a few friendly Fae for the rest of my life?" Evan confirmed.

"Why wouldn't you?" replied Allana.

Evan shrugged, "I don't know. I'm just not sure if maybe this magic food wouldn't go down well for a human." A few moments of silence passed where Evan shovelled the berries into his mouth. Allana was right, they did indeed taste like strawberries. *So she doesn't know basic information about flowers from the human world, but somehow has tasted strawberries enough times to figure out that these berries are really similar?* The odd thought sparked in Evan a desire to learn more about his odd companion. For a few more moments he sat in silence, slowly chewing the berries, deep in thought. Finally, an idea on how to coax Allana into talking about herself popped into mind, and he hesitantly cleared his throat. "So, uh, if you're going to be dragging me around here for a while, shouldn't we tell each other some things about ourselves? You know, like a twenty questions sort of thing?"

Allana glared incredulously at him for several moments, but after a while it drifted into a contemplative look, then to slightly annoyed resignation.

"Fine, we will take turns answering questions, but I am not answering twenty of them." Allana grabbed more berries. "I'll go ahead and answer your first question, yes the berries are fine, you can eat any food of the Fae without consequences." Before Allana finished speaking, Evan had snatched a handful of berries and eaten them ravenously.

"Go ahead with your question," Evan said, his mouth full. Allana turned to face him.

"What's the significance of your necklace? Judging by how much you finger it, it is quite special." Evan swallowed hard, and clutched his necklace, fighting back the ache that had plagued him for months, he answered.

"It's a keepsake, from my grandfather."

Allana looked up at him. He knew there had been a catch in his throat when he answered but he couldn't help that. He had begun to rub at the bullets hanging from his necklace again. He shook his head, shaking away the somber mood he had acquired. "Anyway, it's my turn to ask a question." Evan rubbed his hands together eagerly.

"Oh here we go." Allana muttered, just loud enough for him to hear. Rolling her eyes she raised her eyebrows. Evan took that as a signal to go ahead. "Why do you and the rest of the Fae hate humans so much?" Her eyes widened slightly and her jaw clenched. She composed herself quickly however, and he soon received his answer

"The answers to both of your questions are rather complicated, as there are many reasons why Fae in general hate your kind, but the main reason is that the humans forced the Fae into hiding." Evans' mouth began to open. "And before you ask, no one really knows how they did it, and I certainly don't. My reason for hating your kind is far more complex, so I will simplify; they are the reason I am humiliated by my own people, and the reason I will never be considered truly one of them." Allana looked absentmindedly down at her hands; Evan followed her gaze to see blocks of ice covering them. Swiftly she clenched her fist and the ice shattered. Evan however, was not satisfied by her answer. "What do you mean never—" Allana cut him off.

"We should have left several minutes ago. If you wish to see another of the Courts then you will have to stay silent and refrain from foliage induced fanaticism." Allana brushed her jeans off and started off at a brisk pace. Leaving a wake of frost behind her she jogged forward.

Twigs cracked noisily beneath Evan's fast moving feet. Allana had left him far behind. He was glad she had left a trail of frost glittering in the luminescent light from the trees. He had come to a fork in the trail, and he would've been lost without it. *The humans she interacted with must have been horrible if she's this prejudiced against them. Then again, she lives in a culture that hates us. Maybe she was looking at humans through that lens where interacting with one was considered shameful? Well, I'm going to change her mind, we're not all bad, in fact we're pretty great. The 'taking of land' thing must have happened centuries ago, so she can't hate me for that. I know she won't admit it, but honestly, she seems lonely. She hasn't exactly been the nicest to me, but how can I not feel bad for her if she's as much of an outcast from her society as she says she is? Whether she likes it or not I'm going to be her friend, and maybe after a while she'll be mine.* With this resolve in mind, Evan raced forward, barely noticing the frequent amount of mushroom rings. The wind ruffled his hair and a smile lit his face, he hadn't felt this free from everything in months, and he breathed in deeply the invigorating scent of the woods carried by a pleasantly cool night air.

He rounded a corner and skidded to a halt as billowing purple hair came into view, stopping just centimeters from Allana's heels.

"Took you long enough. Step over here." She gestured to the right of her, and Evan complied. In front of him was a huge ring of toadstools, about three feet in diameter. Coming from a gap in the canopy of trees was a beam of sunlight that shimmered like a curtain of energy. Evan lifted a leg to step inside it.

"Agh!" Allana tisked, throwing her arm in front of him.

"What? We have to step in it to get where we're going don't we?"

"Yes, but you're not connected to a specific season, so if you stepped inside, even with me, we would end up in different places."

"I thought you said we were going to the 'Seasonless,'" Evan argued, but he set his leg back in place. Allana took a deep breath and adopted the tone one would use with a very small child, a tone Evan did not appreciate.

"Yes, but it's called the Seasonless because the location has no particular season, so it's equal ground for each of the Courts. But when you step in, it takes you to a section of market with people from your Court which means that you would be taken to the section with the Courtless."

"Who are the Courtle—"

"Just grab my hand, I have nowhere *near* enough time to explain the Courtless to you." Allana thrust her hand to the side impatiently. *You know what, I'll take this as progress,* Evan thought, and grabbed her hand. Together they stepped inside the mushrooms.

Evan shot forward, growing closer and closer to a blinding light at the end of a giant tunnel of nothingness. Evan's eyes burned and he shut them tight, bracing for impact as the distance from the scintillating light decreased. *Slam!* His body hit something hard and he rolled to the side, his shoulder aching from impact.

"If you're finished rolling around, we need to find you some regular clothing." Her voice wobbled in an odd way. Evan cracked his eye open to see a shockingly blue sky above him. *Wait, wasn't it just nighttime? Honestly, I'd ask Allana, but she'd just scoff at me, and, according to the stuff I've seen here already, changing times is pretty normal.* The bright sky was blotted from his view as Allana loomed over him, a disinterested look on her face. However, it looked almost playful, as if she was desperately trying not to laugh at his landing posture. *So that's why her voice wobbled. She's trying not to laugh at me. Friend-progression experiment number one.* Evan groaned dramatically.

"This is regular clothing." He tried to infuse as much petulance into his voice as possible.

"If you continue to behave as a child, I will leave you here." Through his cracked eye he could see her foot tapping impatiently.

"Why would I change who I am for you?" Evan asked, on the verge of laughter himself.

"You are not injured, get off the ground." Allana's voice hardened, but so did Evan's resolve. *I will make her laugh.*

"Nope, my fragile, inferior human body is broken beyond repair. You'll have to drag me." Evan threw himself onto his back in a spread eagle.

"If I must, I will resort to physical harm," Allana warned, crossing her arms. Her posture and eyes said 'when this is over I will murder you' but her tone was nothing but restrained laughter. So Evan played his last card.

"Come at me White Eyes, I *dare* you to try and move me in this state." He glared comically back at the Fae, trying and failing to keep a grin from spreading ear to ear across his face.

"Fine." Calmly, Allana walked forward and gave him a hearty kick.

"Ugh." Evan let out a breath as her foot slammed into his side. He swayed to the side, but his position stayed the same. "Hmm, I honestly expected worse," Evan said loftily, then prepared for the next blow.

Evan could see Allana's disbelieving face as she stared uncomprehendingly down at him.

"Fine, stay there." Crossing her arms she turned and began to walk away. Evan watched her walk away a good fifty feet, before stopping and turning around again. Grinning cheekily, he waved at her. *This will be interesting,* Evan thought. Straining his eyes he could see her turn rigid and begin stomping back towards him. When she had re-crossed the distance back to him he provoked her.

"Seriously, is that the best you got?" He raised his eyebrows.

"Fine, you leave me no choice." Quickly, she stretched her hand out and slowly raised her arm. Ice bloomed from her fingers and created a sheet beneath him.

"Ah, cold cold, cold!" Evan yelped. With another swipe of her hand she dissipated it, so that he was sitting in a puddle of water. Evan sucked in a breath, but he refused to give in, sensing he was close to victory. She took a wide stance then thrust her arms in a flowing motion making a lane of ice that went on for about fifty feet. Evan began to slide slightly. *Oh dear, Oh dear, oh dear.* Evan tried to stop himself but to no avail. Quickly she expanded the ice beneath him in a slant and before he could react he was sliding.

"Ahh! Allana, stop!" The human howled as he plummeted down the icy path. He was nearing the end of the lane. He was on his back now, limbs waving around, like a turtle flipped on his shell. Evan began looking around for a place to stop but before he could spot one Allana began to run along the ice path, making it longer and curving it.

"Allana stop!"

"Never! You were asking for this!" She yelled. Evan was freezing. His clothes were soaked with melted ice and his body was sliding everywhere. He couldn't stop himself, and his arms and legs flailed in all directions. Then, over his screaming, an odd noise echoed through the field, *Laughter? Wait, Allana, Allana is laughing!"* Evan laughed like a madman, *Yes, I did it!* He felt the odd, magical buzzing that he'd felt before while hiking through Aeternum, as though the magical place itself was celebrating his victory. He wanted to make her laugh again. *Swoosh!* He swooped around a curve.

"Allana stop!" He shouted. He couldn't believe his ears when he heard a playful "Never!" in response. He was so shocked it took him a few minutes to realize when he stopped sliding. Crunching behind him signaled Allana's approach.

"Now will you get off the ground?" She asked, smugness dripping from her voice.

"Alright, you win," he sighed, and stood up, "I'm freezing now."

"You'll warm up once we get you into some superior clothes, besides, you brought that on yourself." Evan began to shiver.

"Don't be so dramatic, it's a short walk to the market. Why don't you distract yourself by observing scenery since you find that so fascinating." Just like that, old Allana returned with her usual look of disdain, and continued walking, leaving him in her wake. He watched her go, feeling the wonderful exhilaration and warmth of the exciting ride and Allana's momentary joy melt away like the icy slide, replaced with an odd heaviness. Sighing, he hiked after her.

Once they reached the market, Evan's jaw dropped. Sprawling before him was a vast lane of booths covered in beautiful icicles, whites and blues of every shade covered the tents. He could feel Allana smirking at his reaction and quickly calmed himself.

"It's nice, I guess," he tried to be aloof but he knew he sounded like an awestruck child.

"Humans. Come, they should have some generic clothing for you." Quickly they made their way to a clothing booth. To Evan, the clothing was in an unfamiliar style, but after further inspection he realized it wasn't particularly odd, just several centuries old. For men there were tough leather jerkins with dark green leaf designs and white shirts that were thick with wool. Next, simple, but warm, brown pants were procured for him. And before he knew it Allana had shoved him into a curtained off dressing area.

* * * * *

Allana waited for him to step out, but after a good ten minutes he was still behind the curtain. *He's not used to these clothes, it'll probably take him a while,* Allana reasoned. Soon after these thoughts floated through her mind, Evan exited the dressing room, looking far more Fae-like now that he wasn't wearing jeans and a T-shirt. Allana turned to speak with the worker of the booth, and caught Evan staring at the Fae. He was obviously trying his best not to look fascinated by the white hair and grey skin of the somewhat lethargic woman behind the table. But he was failing. Allana looked him over again

"Yes that should do," she turned toward the white haired Fae, "If you don't mind I'll change into these clothes here." The Fae nodded and Allana went to the curtained off area.

Safely behind the curtain, Allana allowed herself to rest a moment. As she changed she pondered on the last few hours wanting to laugh at Evan's antics with the flowers. But with that memory also came the remembrance of her own behavior. *Her lip quivered. But she held firm, and repressed her bubbling amusement. Part of her longed to smile back at the cheerful human and chuckle at his corny joking, but clearing her face of all emotion she calmly walked towards him. What would it have been like to be allowed to show that kind of wonder openly, without the mockery of one's peers?* Suddenly the urge to laugh left her completely and her heart was weighed down, as she remembered all the times she had wanted to dance in the flowers just for the wonder of it, and all the joy her childhood had been robbed of due to her upbringing. Sighing, Allana continued dressing, her somber thoughts from the past influencing her current ones. *Nothing but shame will ever be given to those who behave in such a way. I must not bend to those urges. He is a human and deserves all the coldness he receives.* Allana grimaced at herself in the mirror. Her thoughts were harsh even to her cynical mind. She shook her head clenching her jaw then plastered on a well-practiced look of disdain before walking out. Allana re-appeared wearing a long sleeved flowy white shirt beneath a shimmery blue dress that was reminiscent of the night sky. It contrasted with her violet hair beautifully, but the overall style was loose, and provided easy movement. The white haired Fae spoke.

"The ring is just behind the booth." Allana nodded her head and walked straight out of the kiosk without so much as a nod of thanks. As she rounded the outside corner of the booth Allana groaned when she heard Evan yell, ,"Thank you!" She could very easily imagine the scowl he received in return to his rude words..

"Hurry up," Evan hurried out of the booth and circled to the back and sure enough there was a ring of white mushrooms. Allana held out her hand; he took it and soon blinding light overtook them.

Allana breathed the crisp air deeply. Wind was whistling through the woods. As snow blanketed the forest floor, Evan shook his head in amazement.

"But how —"

"It's very complicated and I really don't have time to explain it."

"Oh come on this is so —"

"We need to hurry, days are shorter here."

"Oh, ok." Evan was downcast but Allana ignored him. *Just because I do one fun thing doesn't make him my friend that was a one-time thing. It won't happen again.*

"Why are we stopping here?" Evan asked. Allana raised her eyes to heaven.

"Because there's a personal item I left at my previous home, I've been meaning to retrieve it, since 'I'm supposed to show you around the Courts I decided to take the opportunity to grab it. She explained, quickening her pace.

The snow crunched beneath their feet and silence reigned. As they passed a large pond, memories plagued her. *Yeah a stupid human game.* Allana shook her head and walked faster. He was out of the clearing around the pond when— *Smack!* A deep chill went up her back as anger filled her. She whirled around to see Evan, his arm still extended, his face sheepish. His expression changed to one of maniacal resolve as he shook the remaining frost from his fingers. "It's payback time."

"You. Are. So. Dead." she threatened, then she dropped to the ground and began to create a snowball in a perfect sphere. Before Evan could react, she threw it, hitting him square in the nose.

"Ahchg!" he spluttered, and fell backwards, hands covering his face. Then, against her better judgement, a dazzling smile broke through, one she hadn't worn in many, many years. Briskly brushing herself off, Allana headed in the direction of her former home.After a quick stop at her old abode, in which Evan 'Oo'd and Ahhed' while she grabbed her book. They continued on through the snow, Allana snowballing him anytime he asked a question she deemed had an obvious answer.

"So, where to now?"

Allana waited to respond while Evan dusted bits of snow from his tousled, slightly damp hair.

"The Spring Court. We might as well get the worst over with," replied Allana, tucking a strand of violet hair behind her pointed ear. "At the very least, there isn't anything in there that will cause you to do anything so foolish as your previous activity." The Fae continued to look straight ahead, but a mischievous glint sparkled in her ghostly eyes.

"Bold of you to assume I won't whack you in the back of the head with a bouquet of flowers," retorted Evan with a laugh. "Their thing is flowers, right?"

Allana tried not to, she really did, but a snort of laughter erupted from her. Quickly they hopped into the ring. When the brightness dissipated from their eyes, Allana turned toward him. "As for your question about their 'thing', does this answer it?" She pushed a bushy weed out of the way of his view.

Following the direction of her gesture, Evan peered upwards, astonishment freezing him in his tracks. "Whoa."

Chapter Seven

A pair of golden gates littered with flowers and vines loomed over Evan's head, the entrance to the Spring Court. Glancing over his shoulder slightly, he caught a glimpse of Allana's face. She was staring at the gates with death-like solemnity.

"Oh, come on, you can't honestly say that this isn't amazing."

"Hardly something to be amazed at," she muttered unenthusiastically, "considering the fact it's the entrance into the court with some of the nastiest Fae I've ever known. I guess it must look pretty amazing for an outsider, though." Brushing a strand of hair that had flopped into her eyes back behind her ear, she turned back to the gates. "Come on, I'll tell you a little more about them once we're inside."

As they strode through the gilded gates, Evan couldn't suppress a gasp of astonishment. Flowers. Flowers everywhere. Wherever he turned, they seemed to be decorating every windowsill, lining every street, even growing on the roofs of the buildings. As he paused to gaze around at the endless array of lively colors, he caught sight of a large banner dangling from a nearby pole. A great stag stood against an elaborately designed golden background with roses strewn around its delicate hooves. Evan stood ogling at it for a moment before Allana's voice brought him back from his marveling.

"Come on," she called. "There's a lot more to see than just this."

Evan walked alongside her, burning with what felt like an infinite mound of questions. "So, what's this Court's thing?" he asked. "You know, their power?"

Allana's pale eyes wandered over the lively scene before her, taking in the Fae and scenery around her with undisguised disinterest. "The Spring court has a lot of magical abilities with plants, but the thing they're most known for is shapeshifting into animals. But probably the most important thing you'll need to know about them is they are the most pompous and disagreeable creatures you'll ever meet in your entire short human life."

"Oh, o- okay," Evan responded hesitantly. *Gosh, I really hope I don't get on some Spring Court Fae's bad side. What is that rushing sound? It sounds almost like water.*

"Allana, what is that rushing sound?" he queried, unable to contain his curiosity.

"It's the May Falls. It's a giant waterfall on the hillside. It used to be where the May Queen lived so they made it their capital city. It actually feeds a collection of rivers that run all throughout Aeternum."

"There's a waterfall here!" Excitement filled him, *How beautiful it must be.*

"Hold your horses, we don't have time to go see it. I still have to take you through the Autumn court."

"Bu—"

Evan's attention and response was diverted slightly as a *whoosh* overhead announced the arrival of one of the winged Fae. The Fae landed lightly on the polished cobblestones, adjusting his flower-strewn collar and gazing around with a haughty expression. His wings were highly reminiscent of some of the damselflies that often hovered over the lake near Evan's house, shimmering under the now pleasantly sunny, and cloudless sky. Evan was watching with astonishment as he folded his regal wings when an interesting thought struck him.

"You know, this court kind of reminds me the most of the Fairies from Fairy Tales. I mean Spring and Winter did too, but this one reminds me most out of the courts you've shown me."

He turned back to Allana to see a veiled look of curiosity spreading across her face as they walked along. "What exactly are Fae- er, *Fairies* like in Fairy Tales?" she asked inquisitively.

"They're these tiny, winged people, usually only girls," said Evan. "They're small enough to ride those little horse things we saw earlier." He paused, thinking back to the days when he loved hearing such stories. "Hmm, they also had these sparkly little magic wands that they used to help people and stuff."

Evan glanced up from his pondering to see Allana gawking back at him with a look of disbelieving amusement. "Seriously?" she said, with a slight laugh.

"Yup," replied Evan with a grin.

"So, you avoid showing yourself to humans for a few centuries and suddenly they think you're sparkly twig-wielding insect servants?" she reflected.

"Pretty much," chuckled Evan. He snickered as an idea hit him. "Oh gosh, if you hate that, I'd better not tell you about the tooth fairy."

"The *what?*"

Evan opened his mouth to answer, but was cut off as he nearly walked straight into a large deer. "Oh, I'm so sorry," said Evan apologetically, "I wasn't paying attention to where I was going."

He waited for the deer's response echoing within his own head to come, but no such reply came. Instead, the doe, who'd turned to face him, gave him a nasty glare and huffed loudly. Suddenly, in a whirl of light, the doe was no longer a doe, but a very tall and foreboding Fae woman scowling down at him with a superior expression of annoyance. "Of course you weren't. If I had my way, you scrappy Fae from other courts wouldn't be allowed to come into our beautiful streets and clog them up with your staring, and distasteful form of dress," she growled.

Completely flabbergasted at the Fae's transformation and immediate nasty response, Evan could only stand there, mouth half open in shock. "Well, you don't have your way," interjected Allana coldly. She stepped up to face the scowling and mildly surprised Spring Fae. "And I'm afraid you'll have to find some other unfortunate Fae to vent your opinions on because we are quite busy." And with that, she beckoned to Evan and marched away.

Allana stalked away from the appalled Fae, "Where do they get the idea in their heads that they're somehow so much better than every other Fae?" She asked irritably. Evan assumed the question was rhetorical, but responded anyway.

"Yikes, you weren't kidding when you said they're pompous and prideful. Thanks for getting me out of there."

A flash of irritation spread over Allana's face. "Stop saying that," she responded snippily.

"Stop saying what?" countered Evan, with exasperating oblivion.

"Stop saying thank you. It's so human. " Her face scrunched in disgust. Evan bit back a retort as his eyes caught sight of a magnanimous flower shop.

Evan gazed over the endless array of flowers with awe. A clump of Daffodils burst from a pot, and a row of massive Tulips bloomed from a flower box. He paused his starry-eyed gazing to look at a cheerful-looking Lily of the Valley growing from a vase. *Noel loves these flowers,* Evan thought fondly, feeling a pang of homesickness as he thought about his family. *I wonder when I'll be able to go back home.* Several small flashes of color pulled him out of his reverie. A little herd of the tiny winged horses flapped down to land on a shelf housing several pots of Bluebells. They dispersed, nibbling on some of the weeds that had snuck their way into the soil. Evan grinned, leaning down to get a better look at them. However, one of the tiny creatures, a chestnut-colored one with brilliant vermilion wings, didn't seem as cheerful and curious as its comrades at the idea of this giant creature getting so close. Cantering forward with its head low and ears flat against its head, it nipped Evan rather hard on the nose. "Ouch!" he yelped, jerking back.

His outburst had clearly caught the attention of the store owner. The Fae turned to him with a disdainful and mocking look. "Didn't anyone ever tell you the orange-colored ones are nasty? Honestly, some of you non- Spring Fae can be complete numbskulls."

Slightly abashed, Evan rubbed his bitten nose. "Well, to be fair, I'm not from around here." His attention was slightly diverted as one of the tiny horse creatures flew over to land next to a cluster of beautiful drooping white and yellow flowers. "Wow, do you grow these plants yourself? I don't think I've ever seen a Lutescens in person before, much less one this big and vibrant. My mom's always loved them."

The shop owner's face lapsed from one of distasteful mockery to a slightly more friendly look of immense pride. "I do in fact grow these myself," he said, leaning down to gently scoop up one of the flowers. "Finest flowers in all of Aeternum. I hardly ever get anyone who recognizes what they are though. You know your stuff, kid."

Evan smiled. He could hear Allana calling for him from where she stood away from the bustle of the street. Bidding the store owner farewell with a wave, he ambled over to join Allana. "Finally," she sighed in annoyance, "I was beginning to think I wouldn't even be able to show you the Autumn Court by the end of the day because of how long you were taking." She glanced up at a large clock perched upon a tower across the street. "The crowds here aren't too terrible. We should be able to cut straight through the city to the Autumn

Court with plenty of time to spare." Motioning to Evan to follow, Allana stepped out into the street.

Dodging between people in pursuit of the swiftly walking Fae, Evan tried to both keep an eye on her purple-haired head through the crowd and survey the shops around him. He saw a shop selling some of the most flamboyant clothing he'd ever seen, followed by what appeared to be a pet store selling only peacocks.

"Watch it!" barked an irritable looking Fae as Evan accidentally stepped on their over- shined boot, with several others scowling at him as though a lowlife like himself doing such a thing should be a crime. Evan shrunk back with a hasty apology, glancing around for Allana. A vague sense of panic fluttered in his stomach as he fruitlessly searched the crowd for her. *Maybe I can ask someone,* he thought, *no, there's no way I can do that. Everybody here is too unfriendly.*

Suddenly, an odd voice echoed in his head. *Can I help you? You look a bit overwhelmed.* Evan glanced around for the source of the voice before feeling something gently bump his side. *Over here.*

Glancing down, Evan saw that the source of the voice was clearly a young, kind-eyed stag. "Oh, hello!" said Evan, grateful to hear a welcoming voice. "Sorry about that. With all of this noise, I couldn't figure out who was speaking."

It's quite alright, said the stag, flicking a velvety ear. *Even my keen ears can sometimes struggle with how loud it is here. Anyway, you seemed to be searching for something, and I was wondering if I could be of any assistance.*

"Oh, yeah," replied Evan, "I was looking for a frien- er, companion of mine. Have you by chance seen her? She's got purple hair, she's a Winter Court Fae."

The stag glanced past Evan, flicking his cottony tail. *Is that her over there? That looks like the person you described.*

Whirling around, Evan followed the stag's line of sight. Squinting, he could see Allana glancing around for him at the end of the street. "Oh, yeah, that's her!" He turned back to the deer. "I'd better catch up to her. Thank yo— sorry, it seems like Fae don't really like me saying that. Do you care?"

Not at all, said the deer politely. *"That's a Fae custom. You're very welcome.*

"It was nice meeting you!" Evan called over his shoulder with a grateful smile. He turned and jogged through the crowd until he came within sight of Allana.

"There you are," grumbled Allana testily. "What is with you and getting so incredibly sidetracked?"

"Sorry," mumbled Evan apologetically. "I got lost in the crowd."

"Of course you did. Now come on, and this time, stick close, *please.*"

Slipping down a side road, Evan trailed after Allana as she led him across several more populated streets. Finally, stepping from a rather plain path between two rows of buildings, they came out into a square lined with brilliantly vibrant rose bushes. Pausing to gaze around the area, Evan caught sight of an immaculate marble statue of a young woman with great butterfly wings standing in the middle of the square. At its feet were showered hundreds of colorful flowers, piled so high it's feet weren't visible. As they approached it, Evan pondered over the statue's kind, wise-looking eyes. Though the marble flowers decorating its hair were quite reminiscent of what appeared to be the Spring Court style, the statue's air of kindness seemed unnatural after the snobbery Evan had experienced. "Who is she?" Evan asked, turning to Allana.

Allana didn't answer immediately. She had stopped to gaze into the eyes of the great statue as well, wistfulness showing through her guarded expression. "She was the May Queen," she finally answered. "I believe I told you she was killed by the Fae we thought you might have been. She was a great queen."

Evan hesitated, wanting to ask what had happened, but worried he might upset or offend her. Even under the soft spring sunlight, his fingers had grown slightly cold from the breeze. He stuck his hands into his pockets and felt something soft. Pulling his hand free, he realized that he still had some of the zinnia flowers he'd picked earlier that day. Gently, he laid several of the brilliant pink and salmon flowers on top of the piled high blossoms. As they stood in the warm sunlight of the courtyard, gazing into the marble face of the former ruler, Evan once again became aware of the soft buzzing that filled his ears and tickled his skin. *I wonder if it's from the Fae magic all around this place.*

"Alright," said Allana, seeming to snap out of her reverie. "There isn't much else important to see here, so let's head over to the Autumn Court." Quickly they found a mushroom ring, and stepped through.

"Allana, I thought you said we needed to hurry, why are we in the seasonless?" Evan asked.

"The Seasonless paths are the only way to travel to the other Courts. Long ago the Courts fought amongst themselves and were able to ambush each other very easily by using special rings they had placed in strategic spots. When the May Queen restored order, she created the Seasonless where all of the mushroom rings going just outside to the Court capitals were placed, and it became peaceful ground." Allana explained, with little to no expression in her voice. After winding their way through several more streets, Allana and Evan arrived at a gate. Evan opened his mouth to ask, but Allana cut him off.

"No, this is not the entrance to Autumn Court, they just think gates are pretty." Allana said drolly. As Evan filed this piece of information away and stepped through the gate, he felt the sensation of stepping into an air-conditioned building flood over him. He glanced up in confusion at the sun still shining merrily overhead despite the fact he couldn't feel its rays. *Wait, what? How?* He turned to ask Allana, but she was already stepping into the throng of Fae. Following her, Evan slipped into the crowd. Glancing about, Evan couldn't suppress his awe. One Autumn Court Fae vendor was selling elegantly designed treats that looked to be made of maple syrup, while the shop next to him specialized in all sorts of drums. Several Fae were beating smaller drums outside the shop, shooting nasty glances at the trumpet shop across the street, which seemed to be preparing to put on the same show. The clopping of hooves behind him made Evan glance around, the creature before him making him gasp with excitement. A glistening white unicorn was being led out to an interested buyer, its eyes flashing cheerfully in the sunlight and its ears twitching to take in the bustle around it.

"Come on," called Allana, "I don't want to lose you in the crowd again."

Continuing down the crowded lane, Evan paused at a crooked sign that read 'Bizzare Human Trinkets: buy 1 get 1 free!' Sitting on the table next to it was a broken flip phone, some ancient- looking crocs, and a party hat among many other odd items. *Why would anyone want to buy this?* thought Evan.

As he pondered over the odd items, a Spring Court Fae wandered up to observe the trinkets. Scoffing superiorly, he glared down his nose at the various objects. "I can't believe any of our kind could ever resort to even touching this human rubbish," he snorted. The Fae straightened up with a huff of disgust.

Glancing over his shoulder at Allana, Evan was slightly shocked to see her glaring at the Fae with an expression of resentment, as though he had insulted her. However, a moment later, she seemed to realize he'd noticed her glaring and her face once again lapsed into indifference. "Follow me," she said, "If you don't hurry up we won't be able to visit the Autumn Court before it gets dark."

"You know, you keep saying that, but it hasn't gotten that much darker." Evan pointed out. Allana sighed

"Each Court is a different Season, and the days are longer or shorter depending on which you're in. We're staying in the Autumn Court, before going to Tempest, Aeternum's Capital. The Autumn Court has similar time to Winter, so the days are shorter, which means in a few hours it will be dinner time in Autumn. So if you want to eat, we need to hurry." Allana sent him a side glance that seemed to say, *If you make me miss dinner, You'll become dinner.* Evan stuck his tongue out at her, kept walking.

Evan meandered after Allana as they wove around the Fae congregated in the Seasonless walkway. Traveling off the path, they chose another mushroom ring; Evan was almost used to the odd rush that came from traveling through them. After the usual light show faded away, Evan took in the world around him. Huge maple trees sprawled overhead. Yawning, Evan rubbed a tired eye. If he hadn't been tired before they'd set off, he was now. In spite of his exhaustion, however, he still longed to see more of this strange world. *I can't believe I can somehow be part of a world as amazing as this,* he reflected. He was brought out of his thoughts as a Bronze gleam caught his eye. Glancing up, he took in the gleaming pair of bronze gates wreathed in dying leaves before him.

Allana, who'd walked through the gates without giving them a second glance, jerked her head. "C'mon," she called.

Ambling through the open gates, Evan felt a wave of cool air envelop him as an excitingly chilly breeze ruffled his hair. Suddenly very grateful for the warm Fae clothing he'd been provided, he hurried after Allana. Beyond the threshold of the gate was a stony path shadowed by humongous rich carmine-clad sugar maples. A light stream of beautiful red and orange leaves gently danced through the air and onto the path he and Allana were walking along, and Evan was once again hit with the enchanting feeling of being lost in a breathtaking dream.

"Before you ask, the Autumn Court mostly possesses a lot of wind-related powers, though they do have some connections to certain trees and such. They're also a lot more laid back than the other Courts, so we probably won't have to deal with nasty staring. Of course they still think most humans and those who associate with them, have a lower intelligence capacity, but they won't detest your existence."

"Oh, well, I'm glad to hear that," replied Evan, relieved he would not have to endure any more snarky scoffing. He lapsed into his admiration of the scenery with a sigh.

Great piles of the multicolored leaves lay along the edges of the path, and Evan resisted the urge to dive into one. Suddenly, a flash of orange fur caught his eye a moment before a fluffy creature nearly crashed into his legs. Sitting up, the little red fox gave Evan a look that, had the creature been human, would be a wide grin. Evan laughed. "Hi! I'm guessing you're loving this forest as much as I am, huh?"

The fox didn't answer, merely giving Evan what looked like an enthusiastic yawn before barreling off toward what was clearly an Autumn Court Fae, and presumably his owner. The Fae glanced over at the pair through deep blue eyes, giving them a kind wave. Smiling, Evan waved back. *This place already seems much more friendly than the Spring Court.*

The beautiful maple trees finally receded as Evan and Allana arrived at the end of the path opening up into a leaf strewn and no less beautiful street. Garlands of leaves strung the windowsills of houses, and Evan could spot several wreaths hanging from deep crimson and rich brown doors. Beautiful white banners depicting a fox in a field of heather were scattered on poles throughout the street, fluttering lazily in the crisp, gentle wind. *This whole area kind of reminds me of old-fashion cottages,* pondered Evan, *just more elegant.*

Through the gentle murmur of the township, a commanding yet gentle voice rang out. "Come along, my little Leaflets! We shall be at the Autumn Court Historical Museum soon."

Peering in the direction of the voice, Evan saw a Fae woman leading a line of young children, who looked around six or seven. If Evan could guess, it seemed like they were on some sort of field trip; they were all wearing identical uniform-like clothing. He watched as one of the children, a young boy, paused to crouch beside a broken tree sapling with a sad expression. Grunting with effort, the little boy heaved the young tree upright. Extending a hand, the child seemed to be trying to touch the wound that had caused the tree to break, but the effort of holding up the tree was too much, and it toppled from his arms. Hastily, Evan glanced over his shoulder. Allana was walking slowly down the street, evidently not yet aware of his lagging behind. *I don't want to annoy her anymore,* he thought. However, as he glanced back at the boy making another fruitless attempt to pick up the tree, he knew he couldn't just leave him. He trotted across the street until he was right in front of the child. "Hey," he called. "Er, do you want some help?"

The child looked up, appearing startled. "Oh, yes please! Will you hold the tree up while I fix it?"

"Sure thing," replied Evan, gently grasping the sapling and pulling it upright, unsure of how this child planned on 'fixing' the tree.

The boy gently grasped his hands around the tree's wound, closing his eyes and sighing. Several moments went by, and Evan was beginning to wonder if the young Fae was perhaps pulling his leg. Then, rather suddenly, the child pulled his hands away, glancing up at Evan. "Okay, you can let go now!"

Perplexed, Evan hesitated. "Are you sure?"

"Yup!"

Under the child's eager gaze, Evan gently released the sapling. To his tremendous surprise, the tiny tree stayed firmly upright. Glancing hastily down at the point where the tree had broken, he merely saw a faint scar in its place. "Wow!" he exclaimed. "It's completely healed!"

"I learned how to do that in school," said the little Fae proudly, dusting off his hands and grinning up at Evan, his small, pointed ears and freckled nose pink from the chill in the air. He cocked his head for a moment, a look of wonder in his blue gaze. "Ooh, I like your eye! I don't think I've ever seen a Fae with eyes that color. What Court do you live in?"

Before Evan could think of a response, the teacher's voice rang from across the street. "Leif, come along, don't dawdle!"

"Whoops, I need to go!" squeaked Leif. Before turning to leave, the small Fae turned to Evan with an earnest expression. "I promise I'll remember how you helped me!"

"Oh, uh, okay. Bye!" Evan called after him, bewildered.

As the little boy hurried off to join his group again, Evan turned to see Allana walking back toward him. "Are all humans as distracted as you are?" she said in mild indignation. "Now come on, and this time, at least *tell me* before you get wildly distracted and I have to walk back to get you." Though her tone was irritable, Evan could see a small smile twisting the corners of her mouth.

As they set off walking down the streets, with Evan listening and glancing about at the buildings around him and Allana occasionally providing tidbits of information on the Court, a question burned within his mind. Finally, as they paused to admire the beautiful music of a street musician's violin, he voiced it. "Allana," he said, stuffing his chilly hands into his pockets, "What's the deal with Fae and not saying thank you? Every time I say it, everyone seems to act like I've said something offensive."

Allana bit her lip, a contemplative expression on her face. "Well, let me put it this way: can you remember all of the times you've said thank you to someone and why you've said it?"

"Er, no," replied Evan, confused. *How am I supposed to remember every single time I've thanked someone?*

"There, that's the point. When you humans say thank you to one another for a good deed, you just forgot about it right after, and where's the real thanks in that? In our culture, your gratitude is proved by remembering their good deed and one day repaying them. That's our 'thanks'."

"So I can say 'thank you' once I've re-paid you for the stuff you've done for me?"

"Yes, I guess so," replied Allana. Evan half-expected her to give him a skeptical look, as though she believed he was incapable of ever doing such a thing, but it never came .

He stood there in ponderous silence, contemplating her words. After a moment, Allana spoke, beckoning to Evan. "Come on, the sun's starting to set, and I need to find a new place to stay since, due to its style of security my usual place at Windalore is out of the question."

"Windalore?" Evan asked, the name sounded very elvish, and he half expected to find out that 'The Lord Of The Rings' was actually a history of Aeternum. Allana grinned.

"If you thought the other Courts had fantastical cities you won't believe your eyes when you see Windalore. It's the capital city of the Autumn Court it's a city made in the branches of the Blightwood forest. If the sun wasn't setting I'd let us take a detour, but it's always best to request lodging when your potential host is awake." A forceful wind made the knee-high grass they were wading through ripple and sent Allana's violet locks into a purple frenzy. "You're telling me there is a giant tree city with Fairies and we can't stop to see it?" Evan was aghast, Summer was his favorite season but Autumn was a close second; mostly due to the world's breezy countenance at that time of year, and he couldn't believe he was going to miss exploring the industrial embodiment of his second favorite season.

"That's exactly what I'm saying," Allana confirmed, while desperately trying to tame her wild hair. Evan made a pouty face. Allana laughed.

I can't believe she laughs so much. She used to be so.. Aloof, Evan contemplated, still giving his companion his best pouty face. "Tell you what, later, when all the most powerful Fae in Aeternum don't want you dead, I'll pull some strings and take you to see it."

"Really?" Evan bounced on his toes, practically skipping as he caught up to her.

"You have to stay alive first," Allana reminded him.

"Details, details. Now tell me more about it," Evan demanded, and listened with rapt attention for the rest of the trip.

Chapter Eight

Sighing, Allana looked around. She wished she could have shown Evan the Autumn Court fully. *I have to take him sometime, once the Tablarye crisis is over and the Courts don't want to kill him. Because I am not missing his reaction to Windalore. Maybe I'll find a camera and put a picture of his ridiculous face in my scrapbook.* She smiled at the thought, but the sentimental part of her rebelled. *No! That's only for you and Jay, you can't put photos of friends in there, it's a family scrapbook. And he's not your friend.* Her face fell remembering her brother. But she cast aside her reverie and focused on the task at hand. She needed to find a place to hide Evan while she went to the Court meeting. She knew the Court wouldn't be too welcoming towards him. She didn't know where to go, or where to hide him. She knew she had to conceal him but she couldn't figure out who she could trust to babysit him. The Court had always been this way. They had always been very strict and non-forgiving to anyone, sometimes even their own people if it meant they could protect everyone else. She mostly understood why. She wanted to protect things the way the court protected its people but she also needed to hide Evan from not only them but all of the Shadow Court. She'd never met one until she'd gone to retrieve Evan, and realized that all the horrible stories she'd heard since she was seven were actually true. She knew if the wrong people got their hands on Evan and his powers, he would be executed immediately, and then they'd have an even worse problem on their hands.

As they meandered down the leaf-strewn street, they passed a sweet shop full to the brim with maple syrup treats and fresh-smelling pastries. A colorful art shop stood next to it, full of decorations that Allana guessed young fairies had made. She turned a corner to see the shop she once perused with her friends. It was a very pleasant memory. She thought about the purple dress she got that day when she was shopping, the one she kept for years, the one that matched her long purple hair and white eyes. She could recall the little bunnies stitched ornately into the fabric, and how tracing their threads as she looked at them had brought her such comfort and joy. The memory of the dress she left at home in her closet faded out of her mind as she walked. She looked around the corner of the building she was walking around cautiously, making sure not to let her guard down. She just couldn't risk messing up. Evan was right behind her, looking confused. *He's flabbergasted, like usual.* She continued to walk and then stopped.

"Allana? Are you okay? What's going—" Evan attempted to get answers.

"Uh huh! I know where we will stay tonight." *I can't believe I didn't think of her earlier.*

She pointed straight ahead and sped up a bit, Evan trying to keep up. *I worked with her every day as a queen's maid. Why did it take me this long to think of going to Ember?* She knew that, even though she didn't know Ember terribly well, the Fae could keep an important secret well, and this was definitely very important. She just needed to remember where exactly Ember's small house was. *I'm quite sure it's at the corner of the Autumn Court nearest to the castle. It won't be that far of a walk from here.* "Come on," she called back to Evan, trotting off in the direction of the house.

As the sun was starting to set, Allana took another turn. She saw the castle and knew she was close to where Ember lived. They swiftly passed the castle where the May Queen once ruled. Allana felt a dull pang of sadness stab at her, but tried to not notice it. The thought of all that had happened made her wish she could curl up and forget it all, but life never seemed to work that way. She just missed the May Queen. She missed being there by her side. She longed for the world where the May Queen was still alive. They were steadily growing closer to the castle, walking side by side. Evan kept talking about the different types of birds, but Allana couldn't stop thinking, so eventually Evan's voice faded into the noises of trees swaying in the distance. She looked around at all of the flowers and little insects crawling on the branches of the vermilion, orange, and bright yellow trees. It brought some small comfort to her troubled heart. She could never forget how beautiful this place was. After a while, they saw a pointed roof. She went straight toward it. Once again Evan let her lead and followed her. She went onto the rocky lawn. The blue house looked a bit run down. She hesitated a bit but went up to the door and knocked.

Several long seconds passed, and Allana fought the urge to pace. She could feel the frost creeping across her fingers as they waited. Glancing up at Evan, she saw the human was similarly tense, peering around himself absently and scuffing his feet, his hands deep in his pockets. A volley of muffled footsteps and the click of the door unlocking sounded Ember's arrival. She swung open the door, evidently surprised to see Allana and a teenage human standing on her front porch. She smiled perplexedly and then looked over Allana's shoulder, without saying a word. Her face steadily grew to reflect the anxiety and intensity Allana had felt all morning. After examining Evan for a few moments, she asked, "Now, who's this?" Allana looked at him.

"That's Evan. I'll have to explain everything to you, Ember."

"Yes, yes of course," Ember answered, ushering them both vigorously into her home, looking equal parts very worried and very curious. As they went inside, they both looked around the house. It looked normal, for the most part. Except for the big painting in the kitchen of a cow in an expanse of dying grass and autumn leaves. Evan noticed this as well, and looked at Allana incredulously. Though the majority of her face stayed deadpan as usual, Evan thought he saw the corner of her mouth twitch. Ember asked Allana to come sit by her.

"Hey, Ember, could Ev — er, the human wait in the kitchen while we talk?" Allana answered Ember. Their host nodded, and without looking back the two strode into the next room.

Evan stepped into the kitchen and Allana shut the door behind him.

"Right, I know it's short notice, but you were the only Fae I could think of that would be willing to house him. And, me, since I brought him here," Allana stuttered on the last words, wishing they weren't true.

"Bless your heart, Allana, you're always welcome and having a slower mental capacity is no reason to shun someone. You two can stay as long as you need," Ember responded with a deprecating smile. Confused noises could be heard coming from the kitchen and Ember shouted, "Go ahead and make yourself at home. Don't worry, they will make you tea and a snack."

"They?" Evan shouted back.

"Why, the dishes, of course. Ah, humans," Ember chuckled and Allana rolled her eyes, "Gah!" Evan yelled again and a crash responded form the kitchen. Allana leaped up with Ember right behind her and pushed the door open to see Evan, trying to look like everything was fine, and failing. Soup was in the bowls but the ladle was on the ground. He grinned sheepishly at them. "Sorry, I uh, freaked out a little," he explained.

"Per usual," Allana responded before she and Ember sat down at the table beside him.

"So, you're Evan, huh?"

Evan nodded his head and smiled at Ember. She grabbed the floating soup and bowls and gave some to Allana and placed some soup in a bowl in front of herself. They sat in silence while eating and sipping the chamomile tea that

Ember 's kitchen items had made. It was quite obvious that everything in her house obeyed her. One flick of her hand and all the bowls would move.

As they sat in silence, Allana noticed Evan was analyzing Ember. She had a round face and ocean- blue eyes that looked rather dull and tired, as though from lack of sleep or stress. The work of a maid was quite tiring and Allana hoped they wouldn't be too much trouble for her. She wore a dress, orange colored with tiny flowers and fabric golden leaves sewn all over it. It matched her table. As they finished their meal, Allana spoke. "Ember, it's wonderful that you're doing this for us. I promise I will repay you one day."

"Of course," responded the Autumn Court Fae in her quiet voice. "The entirety of Aeternum could be dependent on this."

Allana smiled slightly, "Is it alright if I speak to Evan in the living room?"

"Of course. I'll clean up while you two chat."

Allana beckoned him into the next room and, as Evan got up from the chair, the bowl floated to the sink right beside the iron- colored pot that had opened by itself a few minutes earlier. Allana then followed him into the living room where Evan sat down on the brown couch. A tiny coffee table sat to the left of the couch, and Allana sat down next to him, positioning herself closely to the side table. A slight clanging in the kitchen alerted them of Ember cleaning up.

"So, Evan, listen. I told her about everything so you don't have to worry. She will let us stay here for a bit. She's very sweet, trust me."

"Alright. Thanks, Allana- I mean," Evan chuckled, "I can't help but say thank you."

Allana narrowed her eyes severely but let a smile stretch across her face and breathed out of her nose. Evan chuckled.

"Man, this still feels like a weird dream," reflected Evan, "I mean, in the last little while I've been chased by a crazy shadowy magic person, teleported into another world, and learned that I somehow have Fae powers."

"Agreed," replied Allana, "This has been a really strange day for me as well, so I can't imagine how mind boggling it must be for a human."

"Yeah," said Evan faintly. Allana watched his face; he seemed to be warring with himself when words burst from his mouth. "What does it mean for me that I have Fae powers? Are people— sorry, I meant Fae, relying on me? If so, how will I be able to help them if I'm just— well, just me?" He dropped his gaze.

A long and tense silence seemed to stretch between them before Allana responded. "I really don't know what this all means yet. Let's just cross that bridge when we come to it.For now, let's get a good night's rest, and figure out what our next course of action will be in the morning."

"Okay," replied Evan, even though she didn't have much comfort to offer him, "Gosh, I don't know how you're able to think that clearly with all of this. I don't do so well under pressure."

Allana looked back at him with a slight shrug. "Well, I guess it comes with being a queen's maid. Even in a smaller position like that, there's a lot of pressure involved with court manners and image and all."

"You were a Queen's Maid! Then were those Spring Court people jerks to you? Why did you say you were rejected by your people? The Queen obviously trusted you shouldn't that have been enough?" Evan exclaimed indignantly. Allana smiled slightly at his innocent indignation.

"The answer is a very complicated one. But as far as the Queen goes, she was a special case among Fae, and was one of a small number that truly treated me as an equal." Allana tried to squeeze emotion out of her voice when she answered.

" I bet you have some pretty dramatic stories from a position like that," replied Evan, grinning.

Allana snorted amusedly, rolling her eyes. "Oh, you have *no* idea."

Evan laughed. "I'll bet the Spring Court was involved in a lot of them, right?"

"Don't even get me started."

Allana felt something she hadn't felt in a long time. Comfort. The feeling she longed for ever since she'd arrived in Aeternum, the ability to enjoy life. She did miss that feeling. A lot. The smile faded from her face. No, she couldn't have any sort of sympathy toward a mere human. *A human! No way.* She tried to shake away the happiness and comfort that she longed for. She wanted it, but she didn't want to experience it from a human. *Even if it's a human that has powers of some sort that could be related to the Shadow Court, which is obviously not of the human world.* She wished she could banish the feeling of the growing companionship with the boy from her mind. Digging her fingernails into her palm, she got up from the couch.

"Hey, I got to go to the bathroom. I'll be right back. Sorry."

Evan nodded his head and Allana went to the left of the room to a door that led to a hallway. She still remembered the layout of the house from the few times she'd been here. As she went into the bathroom, she shut the door and locked it. Sitting down on the edge of the tub, she took a deep breath in and out. She couldn't let herself feel any sympathy for a human. She just couldn't. *Get a hold of yourself.* She got up from the tub and unlocked the door. She went through the hallway to the living room and sat next to Evan once again. He asked if everything was okay and she quickly answered yes while nodding her head.

Ember had made a bed on the couch for Evan and led Allana to the guest bedroom. It was small and slightly plain, though still charming in its own way. A beautiful pattern of golden maple leaves were painted along the walls, as though they were being carried by the wind. Pretty white curtains hung over the big glass window standing above the crimson-blanketed bed, and a worn wooden dresser sat against the opposite wall.

As she gazed about at the calming fall colors, she found herself thinking about the first time she'd entered the Autumn Court. She'd played along with the other children as they scoffed about "how much of an eyesore" the place was for fear of being mocked more than usual, though secretly she'd found the warm, friendly colors beautiful and comforting to look at. *Not that I ever could have said it aloud.* She shook off her thoughts, pulled open the covers and hopped onto the mattress. Right when she was about to fall asleep she heard a furious knock come from the front door. The night air that was once peaceful and quiet was filled with angry voices and whispers. It sounded like there were about three people talking amongst each other. She stumbled groggily out of bed and headed for the hallway where she saw that Ember had also gotten out of bed, followed by a bleary- eyed Evan from the living room. He looked dazed and confused. They all looked to the door, where the angry voices had fallen to a whisper.

Ember then muttered quietly and softly towards her and Evan, "I'll answer the door, just in case." They both watched her walk through the long hallway and look behind her at them. Even from afar, Allana could see her hand shaking as it reached for the knob, unlocking it. While hesitating to open the door, Ember mouthed the word "hide" and Allana pulled Evan with her into a closet in the hallway.

Allana could feel Evan shaking next to her. The closet was cramped, and though she knew they were quiet, their breathing sounded like a hurricane to her sensitive ears. *I hope Ember doesn't suffer because of this.* The wait seemed endless as deep voices talked to her friend. Through the closet door Allana strained her ears to catch the words coming from Ember's voice and a lower one coming from the hallway. She could hear the words "Shadow Court" and "human. She jolted back, got up from where she was and grabbed Evan's shoulder so hard, he almost fell over. She was trying to think about how they could have possibly found out they were hiding here. *They must have followed us, or tracked Evan. We have to get out of here.* Silently, Allana pulled Evan out of the closet and through the hallway. Just as they crept out of the corridor, from the corner of her eye she could see a tall man, black hair covering half of his face, looking right at them. At that moment, she knew they had to run. But the gaze of the Shadow Fae made her freeze. The man started walking forward and Allana scrambled backwards into the guest room. Ember tried to stop him, "Uh, sir! Please don't go back there!" Ember's voice echoed through the house as the operative went through the hallway, his black boots making the floor shake after every step.

"I saw him. I saw someone." His voice was low, filled with rage. Allana and Evan listened as the man searched every inch of the hallway where they had been seconds before. Allana looked at Evan, somehow able to see his outline through the darkness. He was white with terror. She heard the Fae's heavy, furious breathing, as though he were a bull about to charge. A hesitant scuffling alerted him of Ember approaching.

"S-sir, I'm n-not sure what you're looking for h-here, but—"

A horribly loud thud rang out, evidently the result of the operative's fist slamming the wall. Ember let out a breathless squeak, sounding as if she were in tears.

Allana felt Evan tense even tighter next to her and silently begged him not to move. *I want to help her as much as you do, but if you give us away we're all dead..*

The Shadow Court Fae's grumbling snarl filled the air again, "Burn this place down."

"But sir," said another, slightly higher voice in astonishment, evidently another operative, "what about this lady? She's just—"

"Burn it down, now! That's an order!"

* * * * *

Evan's head was lowered and he shook, with fear and remorse, *I brought them here, They tracked me the way Allana did.* The guest room door swung open, and Evan's head snapped up. He looked worriedly at the door and let out a breath of relief when it revealed a violently shaking and tear-streaked Ember, who beckoned them furiously. The trio dashed wordlessly through the house, heading for the back door. *Oh gosh, I really hope they're not waiting outside,* Evan thought with rising panic. Then, the acrid stench of smoke scorched his nostrils, and he found himself staring in horror at the back door, now enveloped in flames. *We're not gonna make it out!* Evan thought, his breath hitching in his throat. He coughed heavily on the smoke. The Shadow Court Fae were yelling at each other.

"Idiot, if we set it on fire they have time to escape!" The heat was all consuming. If someone said his skin was melting off he would have believed them. His eyes streamed, and his vision blurred. Where had Allana and Ember gone? One moment they were leading him to the way out, the next they were gone. Coughs wracked his body, and his lungs ached. *Where are they? And if those Shadow people came back in, why haven't they done anything yet?* "Allana," he tried to shout, but his smoke filled throat constricted his volume and it came out as a croak.

Evan couldn't help it. He panicked. He started running, shouting for his friends, desperate to escape the phosphoric atmosphere. While running, Evan looked back and saw the huge hole that mysterious operative punched into the wall. He felt himself shiver. The Fae must have been very powerful. He wished he had never come to this place.The smoke was making him lightheaded. Guilt plagued him. Her house. Burnt down, crumbling, now abandoned. All because of him. *All I've done is come here and become a problem to these people, and now look at what's happened. All because I can't do anything but be a useless burden.* A deafening *crack* rang out from above him, and Evan jerked his head up to see the ceiling crumbling, tumbling toward him like something out of a nightmare. Unable to scream, he jerked his hands up in some involuntary motion, as though he could hold the burning wood back from crushing him. Blackness suddenly exploded before him, though he only had a fraction of a second to register it before it all crumbled on top of him. As his world spun toward blackness and a crushing feeling seemed to envelop him, he thought of his companions and if they might be suffering a similar fate. *Goodbye, I'm sorry. Please forgive me.* He hoped Ember could forgive him, and slowly his world went black. *He really was sorry.*

Chapter Nine

Evan opened his eyes to complete chaos. Debris was falling and his lungs ached from coughing up dust. He searched frantically but Allana and her friend were nowhere to be seen. Evan shoved a board off his torso and struggled to stand up. *The fire stopped. How? You know what, that doesn't matter. I have to find Allana.* Once on his feet, he began a more thorough search for his friends.

"Allana, Ember, where are you?" he coughed. Panic was rising in his throat, and he wanted to shout louder for them, but his smoke- coated throat could barely manage anything more than a hoarse croak. Peering about, he squinted in an attempt to see the outline of his friend. It was pitch black, and the crumbling building made vision impossible.

"Over here," the voice was tired, almost lethargic, as if the words had been forced through a yawn. *That must be Allana. She was still groggy when they crashed in here.* He wanted to race forward to see if she was ok, but the dark and debris prevented him. *If I just had a flashlight… I can't go any faster than this because if I do I'll trip over something and break my neck.* Vaguely he saw the outline of a person, somehow it felt as if the closer he got to her, the murkier it became. He reached out to put a hand on her shoulder. Claw like fingers shot forward and grabbed his wrist. Her head turned and the shadows moved. Suddenly he could see an evil grin glittering at him. *That's not Allana..* Evan yanked his arm back, but the hand gripped him like iron.

"Let go!" he yelled, but it was no use, the smile was moving toward him and slowly his body was pulled forward.

"It seems Veratyrr was right, you do have shadow powers. No matter, once you're gone and your power transfers to him, taking the rest of the Courts will be child's play. Especially now that their precious May Queen is dead." The Shadowy assailant snorted in cruel laughter, leering down at Evan. "It really was obscenely easy for him to kill her, not a single bit of resistance. I wonder what he'll give me for killing you." The voice was cold and gravelly, and it grated against Evan's nerves in an oddly familiar way.

Evan could feel warm breath against his face and he gagged at the stench of it. He had ceased struggling, the closer the Shadow man came the more paralized he felt. *I have to get away. That Verrytyrr dude is the one Allana's been looking for. If I just say something maybe I could get her attention –* "Goodbye Evan Hale," the voice whispered. Suddenly Evan realized why the voice was familiar, as only one person had ever called him by his full name. *Elmer Gristle.* A shadowy sword appeared. Time seemed to slow as the blade was thrust upwards and slowly came down.

Evan's body felt strange, like all the adrenaline within him was rushing into his forearms and building up, waiting to explode forward. His arms twitched, the blade was inches from his body. *Woosh!* Blackness thrust out of him, Elmer was forced backwards and the sword dropped from his hand. Evan leaped out of the way of the falling sword. He felt strangely drained, but he didn't stop to consider it as he sprinted through the crumbling house. Suddenly, he could see everything. It was a weird sort of vision, everything was coated in a murky darkness, it was similar to night vision goggles, everything was outlined with dark shadow lines that contrasted against the dim starlight. *Starlight? Elmer must have been making it darker than it really is, using his freaky shadowness.* Using his newly enhanced sight, he spotted the form of a person. He didn't rush forward this time, he stayed a few feet away.

"Allana?" he questioned cautiously, "If it's you, do something icy." Snowflakes covered him in an instant. "Not that icy!" Evan shivered and began to brush the snow off.

"I told Ember to go get reinforcements to capture these guys, I managed to subdue one but there were more."

"I know, my neighbor tried to kill me! He pretended to be you and I was going to find you and then he tried to stab me and-" Evan's voice was rising in pitch. Allana slapped her hand over his mouth. Evan grunted in surprise, and his mouth stung.

"We have to go, and if you keep shouting he's going to find us, come on." She snatched up his hand and, following her lead, they raced out of the hole in the wall and headed in the direction of the castle.

Evan breathed hard, the cool spring air stung his throat and his lungs burned. *I wish she would slow down, my hand hurts from gripping so tight.* Evan hadn't let go of Allana's hand since she'd dragged him out of the collapsing building an hour earlier, if anything he'd squeezed harder. Whatever the Shadow operative had done to him had shaken him to the core. Evan raced forward but his body was giving out, his pace slowed down more and more until his legs refused to go and he screeched to a stop.

"Ach!" Allana gasped in front of him as her body was jerked back from his sudden stop. Evan leaned over, hands on his knees, taking huge wheezing breaths. He opened his mouth to say something but shook his head and took another breath instead. After a moment or two he managed to force out,

"Th—" he took a breath. "The adrenaline is wearing off. I don't know how my Granddad went through situations like that all the time. I can't run like this for much longer." He straightened, and panic creeped into him again.

"You don't have to run like *this*, *this* isn't even running. You have to run like you were," Allana smiled slightly. Evan chuckled, "Hehheh, was that a joke? From you of all people. Sorry, you of all Fae, not people," Evan was too tired to think straight, and wasn't quite sure he had heard her right.

"Come on, we should be at the castle in less than a mile, and yes it was a joke. If you must know, I'm not cold all the time. On occasion I can almost be at room temperature." Evan was incredulous, then, unable to control himself he let out a loud set of guffaws.

"That was amazing!"

"Well, contemplate its genius while we run, because either your neighbor is right on our tail or he's gone to report to his leader. Both choices give us a small amount of time," she grabbed his hand and raced forward, dragging him behind her until, much to his relief; he was able to keep up.

Evan gasped. Before them were massive golden gates, behind the entrance was an enormous stone castle, with towers reaching for the sky at each corner, and turrets scattered throughout. The roof of each section was gilded in gold. "Evan, come on. Once we're in the gate we can relax," Allana persisted

"What?" Evan shook his head.

"I know it's huge, gaudy and distracting, but you can gawk at it once we're inside." she insisted

A shadowy figure stood just behind the gate.

"Allana, thank goodness you're ok! The courts didn't believe me."

"Of course they didn't, they don't believe anything can mar the perfect little world they think they created," Allana grumbled. Evan was still too awestruck to greet their friend. The gate swung open and they rushed in.

"Uh, does that mean they're gonna suspect me?" Evan asked, hesitation to enter the castle seizing him. "It's either them or the Shadow Court Operatives," Ember responded, ushering them forward as she did so.

"Much as I hate to admit it, in this instance, the Spring Court is the lesser of the two evils," Allana said, then quickly strode down the lane.

"I thought you said once we were in the gate we could relax," Evan complained, and smiled when he saw her raise her eyes to heaven.

"Let me put it to you this way. I brought you here. If you sleep outside, I am obligated to make sure you don't do anything stupid for the whole night, which means I'd have to sleep on the ground. Tell me Evan, what do you think would happen to you if I was robbed of my nice comfortable mattress because you couldn't walk ten feet?" Allana was smiling, her teeth glinted ominously in the moonlight, and there was an evil gleam in her eye.

Evan gulped, and quickened his pace. Allana smirked. They kept silent until they reached the castle entrance

Allana knocked hard on the grand cherry wood doors. On either side of the door, was a peach tree, white and pink buds in full blossom. By some magic the branches crawled up the sides of the door like vines and the flowers decorated the front of the regal entrance. In moments the doors swung open, the branches acting as silent hinges. In front of them was a Spring Court Fae wearing a beautiful dress. The bodice was made of a soft sky blue material that was fitted at the waist. The skirt was made entirely of giant, dinner plate- sized hibiscus petals with deep magenta at the ends that faded to sky blue then to orange and finally yellow. The skirt was large, and a three foot train dragged behind her graceful footsteps. Her delicate face was framed by a textured bob and gentle blue eyes shone behind her wavy blonde hair. She rushed forward and swept Allana into a massive hug.

"Allana! I'm so glad you're ok. I believed Ember but none of those pompous windbags did." She squeezed tighter.

Evan watched this interaction with amazement; he'd never seen someone so graceful and beautiful before.

"It's good to see you too Thea, but — I can't breathe," Allana gasped.

"Oh sorry." Thea quickly released her. Allana turned around and chided him."Evan, don't be rude, and say hello like a polite little human."

"Uh… I'-I'm Evan. It's nice to meet you.. M'lady."

"Oh good grief, at this rate I'm going to have to invest in some blinders for you," Allana muttered, just loud enough that Evan heard her. *How am I supposed to know how to talk to her? She's pretty enough to be a royal person*, Evan thought indignantly. Thea laughed.

"My Lady? Honey, I'm a maid. A High Court member wouldn't be caught dead wearing this old thing. It's over a century old. Come on, you're obviously tired, why don't I show you where you'll be sleeping and you can tell the courts all about your exploits in the morning." She turned and led the way down a long corridor took a couple of turns and stopped at a door with an engraved snowflake on it.

"Here, Allana, you can sleep here and the human, Evan, was it? Can sleep in the room next to yours."

"Thank you," Evan said, not sure whether he should go into his room or not he stood awkwardly to the side as Allana exchanged words with her friend.

"Thea, I'm really glad you were the one to greet us instead of — Someone less pleasant."

"You can say it, I know you're glad it wasn't one of my fellow Court members. Everyone hates them, they're jerks. Even those of us who interact with them on a regular basis dislike them heavily. The difference is I understand how they got to be that way." Thea smiled softly while she said this and Allana leaped forward and hugged her.

"I've missed you so much."

"The feeling is mutual. Now go to sleep. If you are to have the strength to deal with Hyacinth you must rest."

"Truer words were never spoken," Allana laughed and walked towards her room. "Evan, you can go to sleep now," Allana told him.

"Oh, good, I didn't know if it was rude to go while she was still here," Evan explained and walked into his room glad to go to bed.

Evan was restless. His body was exhausted, but his brain wouldn't shut up. Something was bugging him about his encounter with Elmer and his upper story was a mess with possibilities. *He tried to kill you, you're probably just in shock still, that has to be it, because other than that I have no idea what it could be.* This somewhat settled him, but it was many hours before he managed to sink into sleep, and even then true rest was elusive.

"Let go!" he yelled, but it was no use, the smile was moving toward him and slowly his body was pulled forward.

I wonder what he'll give me for killing you." The voice was cold and gravelly, and it grated against Evan's nerves in an oddly familiar way. Evan twisted in his bed, the sheets tangling furiously. "Goodbye Evan Hale," The voice whispered. Elmer… all the adrenaline in his body was rushing into his forearms and building up waiting to explode forward, his arms twitched, the blade was inches from his body. Woosh! Blackness thrust out of him, Elmer was forced backwards and the sword dropped from his hand. Over and over the scenario played, every time more vivid than the last. Suddenly it changed. *Bullets whizzed by his ears and men in military uniforms were everywhere. Sitting against an embankment next to him was a man with mussed brown hair and hazel eyes. Laser focused on the approaching enemy, he let out round after round of bullets into the air. The previously advancing men began to retreat and Evan's mouth moved of its own accord.*

"We're pushing them back Jackie!"

"They must have caught sight of your devilish face peeking over the embankme – " **Boom.** *dust flew in the air and both Jack and*

Evan flew through the air. His ears rang and right before he hit the ground; adrenaline seemed to explode out of his body and a dark haze surrounded him. Pain flared everywhere, his lungs ached and vaguely he realized a bomb must have been thrown on them. Them... Jack, he had to find Jack. Frantically he looked to his right, his body ached and the pain was accentuated by the quickness of his movements. He almost didn't recognize him, so horrific was the twisted shape of Jack's body. No.. no... no... tears streamed down his face as he slowly managed to crawl over to Jack's body. He laid his head on his friend's chest and wept whispering "Why wasn't it me? Why wasn't it me..." with this last word his world went black.

"Jack!" Evan shot up in bed, energy rushing through him. Light streamed in from the window, but he hardly noticed, so deep was his distress. "Why me?" Evan muttered, hugging his knees to his chest. "Wait a minute, Jack, was Grandpa's friend the one — The one that died right next to him? the one that made him guilty?" *Why did I dream about that story?*

Thump. Thump. Thump. From the door. Evan jerked upright, covering his head with his arms. The *'Booms'* in his nightmare, still vivid. Then a voice came through the door.

"The meeting is starting soon, you need to get up."

"Uh.. O-Ok, I-I'm coming." Evan couldn't get the image of Jack's decimated body out of his mind. *And I only dreamed about it, how much worse would it be if I had been there?* He shook his head, he wanted to come off as normal as possible so Allana wouldn't question him too closely. He heard ice crack outside his door. Smiling slightly, Evan untangled himself from his blanket cocoon, struggled into his Fae clothing, and opened the door. Sure enough, ice shards were melting on the floor. "You really do need to warm up Allana," Evan admonished.

"Oh, shush," she snapped, and walked ahead of him. *Verytyrr, I need to tell her about him! I can't believe I forgot.*

"Uh Allana, when Elmer tried to stab me, he went on a bit of a monologue. And—" Allana whirled around.

"What did he say?" Her white eyes bored into him.

"He- he said that this guy named Vera- uhh- Veratyrr he wanted t-to kill me to get that excess power stuff you and Athena talked about, and that he's, he's the one who murdered the Queen." The last part came out in almost a whisper.

"That little— ugh! We thought it was Tablarye which is why we tracked him to you but it's his son. And if you have the excess power, that means Tablarye is really dead. We have to get to the meeting now." And with that, Allana swept off, a new, Cherry blossom dress trailing out behind her.

Magnificently decorated halls surrounded him, with enormous pink flowers and gold appearing to be a running theme. Much as he wanted to take in the splendor, all of his concentration was focused on not losing sight of Allana, or rather the flurrying ends of her white skirt.

At last they reached the doors that led to the conference room. Evan panted behind her. *I really need to get in shape.* Halting just behind her, Evan saw Allana take a deep breath before swinging the large wooden doors open. The room was large with a high domed ceiling that glittered gold. Wooden seats were separated into four sections, with a polished stone pathway leading between each section. In the east corner was the Spring Court, each row of seats had a peach tree canopy and the benches were covered in petals. In the corner adjacent was the Summer Court corner and, unlike the rest of the sections, it did not have something particularly connected to their magic, instead one set of benches had percussion instruments such as drums, while the other side had long golden trumpets. The side with trumpets had a dolphin flag at the end of the benches, and the Percussion side had a flag with a horse on it.

In the opposing corners were Winter and Fall. In Winter, icicles and frost covered everything and ice sculptures of lynxes sat on either end of the benches. Fall had a maple tree at the end of each row and each tree's leaves were a beautiful ombre of orange, red, and yellow. Leaves dotted the floor, and the benches had intricate carvings of wind and foxes. At the back of each corner was a door, and all except Summer had their flag hanging on it. For Fall, a fox turning into autumn leaves that were blown in the wind against a white background. For Winter, a Lynx prowling in the snow. Spring had a leaping stag with flowers twisted around its antlers. Squaring her shoulders, Allana made her way to the Winter Court section and Evan followed. Sitting, they watched as the doors in each corner opened.

Evan caught his breath as streams of impeccably dressed Fae entered the glorious room. The Summer Court Fae, including Athena, arrived in a gaggle and were already talking amongst themselves. Their wings were like stained glass butterfly wings. The sunlight streamed through them and spilled vibrant colors across the floor.

"Wait, they have wi—" Allana slapped her hand over his mouth.

"Yes, now shut up. You're not supposed to talk until all of the Courts are present."

"But they—"

"I'll explain later, now hush," Allana hissed, keeping her hand firmly over his mouth. Evan tapped her hand twice and looked pleadingly at her. Allana sighed, and hesitantly removed her hand. Stretching his jaw, Evan looked to his left and saw the Autumn Court enter in pairs of two. They walked to the back of the last bench together then separated and flew down to the front and sat next to each other in the center of the front bench. This repeated until each bench was filled with Fae. *Huh, with how they're all dressed it almost looks like fall leaves.* Next came the Winter Court Fae. They trooped out in groups of eight. Each group walked single file towards the next open bench and sat one at a time until the benches were filled. Like Allana, their skin was gray in complexion, and all had varying versions of white, blue, and purple features. Some with ice blue eyes and white hair or vice versa, but it appeared that none had the same Purple and white eyed combination that Allana did. When the last group of eight came out and saw that two people were already there, glares and grumbles were exchanged before they squished onto the bench. Then came the Spring Court Fae.

The door was flung open, a collective eye roll went around the room as each member took a long dramatic walk to their seat, like peacocks in their arrogance. All different ranges of style had been shown but nothing was more ridiculous or gaudier than what the Spring Court members wore. Obscenely tall hats of obnoxious colors, skirts that were stupendously puffy, made from huge rose petals that draped over each other, out gracefully as Thea's did, for they were far too fat for that, rather it gave the appearance that they had cut out the middle of a flower and turned it upside down,then made it a skirt. Evan stifled a snicker. Allana elbowed him in the gut, and pain exploded in his abdomen.``Oof." Allana glared. *That is soooo on her, she's the one who elbowed me. Anyone would laugh at those horrible dresses.*

Finally they were all seated and a Spring Court Fae from the front row flew to the front of the room.

"Hecghm. This meeting is officially in session, who would like to start?" A roar of unintelligible noise including drums and horns came from the Summer Court, and an audible groan went around the room., but nonetheless the Fae in the center made a go ahead gesture before leaving the middle and sitting back down. An excited-looking man flew forwards, a trumpet hanging off a strap around his shoulder, a drum hanging from his belt and two flags were in his hands.

He began to speak but before Evan could make out what he was saying Allana started whispering.

"Well, looks like I can explain now, the reason they have wings is because—"

"Shh, I'm trying to listen." Evan strained his ears but a Summer Court Fae without wings had started tapping his drum and it drowned out the speaker. He had a crazed look in his eyes as he focused intently on drumming. Tap-tap-tap, on and on it went.

"Evan, it's just the Summer Court's age- old argument amongst themselves, there's no point in listening. The reason they hav—"

"Why doesn't the crazy drum tapper dude have wings?"

"Who, Mcdougal? He's not a Fae. He was wandering around this building one day, no one knows how he got in, and he got hold of one of the drums. He could keep such a steady beat they basically adopted him. Usually the other Courts would try to get rid of him, but now we don't have to hear about how drums are obviously less tasteful than horns because there's *one* more horn player than there is drummers." Allana rolled her eyes.

"Oh sure. He gets to stay and play his drum while I'm on trial for murder when I didn't even know this place existed!"

"Oh, cry me a river."

"Don't tempt me." Evan turned back towards the Summer Court man, he was waving a trumpet in one hand and a drum in the other.

"The point is, the rest of you have had this sorted out for centuries, and you offer no advice on which we should choose." Evan raised his hand, Allana almost leaped from her chair in an attempt to shove his arm back down, but it was too late, Evan had already started speaking.

"I personally like the drums."

Chapter Ten

Evan looked over at Allana, who now had a hand on her face, shaking her head. Sighing, Evan exchanged glances with Athena from across the room, her eyes sparkled and her mouth twitched in amusement. Evan glared at her, then watched as Allana stood. Now everyone was staring, glaring was more like it, as Allana took a deep breath and spoke.

"Forgive the interruption. I was going to wait for the time allotted for the May Queen discussion to introduce him, but since this matter is slightly more important than the previous topic, I will explain," Allana said, with a deep sigh.

"Go on,"

"As most of you know, I was tasked with searching for the murderer of Ro- The May Queen. Initially my search led me to this human, Evan. He has the appropriate powers, but was rather oblivious. After que—"

"So this is the Murderer? And he dares to give his suggestion to us." The Summer Court Fae raised his head in the air, indignation flowing from him. "Bring him forward."

"No, if you would let me finish I—"

Before Allana could even finish her sentence, the menacingly elegant form of Hyacinth stood from his seat. "Allana, we are aware of your, hmm.. How shall I put it? Situation, with humans, and as such it would be safe for us to assume that a criminal such as this will have weaseled his way into your affections using your rather obvious compromisability. As such, most things you say in his defense will therefore have no effect. "Hyacinth walked slowly across the room, his words looked as if they bothered Allana. Evan felt his face go red. Allana shook her head, while he shifted his legs. Evan could tell Allana was thinking hard, as to not screw up anything said. Hyacinth grabbed Evan by the arm and led him to the center. Athena stood.

"Hyacinth," she began. Despite holding herself high, Evan could hear the hesitance in her voice. "Let us remember that, even in our distaste for this, er, *creature,* that we must follow due process in examining the information provided."

Hyacinth glanced up at the Summer Court Fae, glowering at her in what almost looked to be an unspoken challenge. However, Athena did not drop her gaze, and the Spring Court Fae relented. "Very well, though I couldn't possibly see how a petulant little human with Shadow Heir powers could possibly be anything other than the culprit."

* * * * *

Evan panicked as he was led forward. He looked to Allana for help, but Hyacinth's words seemed to have affected her, and the emotionless expression she had carried for most of their journey returned. *I am never planting Hyacinths in mom's garden ever again.* Athena continued to speak and He whipped his head toward her hoping she could save him.

"Yes, Evan has shadow powers, but the rest of you Skynjari will be able to tell that he only has the excess power of a Court Leader and nowhere near the amount of power Tablarye had. Now, Allana I was told you had more information?" Athena turned to her, and Allana nodded her thanks.

"Last night we stopped at Ember's cottage, and in the night four shadow operatives attacked. If you need proof you can look at the damage done to her house. The fact that Evan is human came in handy. They didn't think he would live long enough to give away the information they revealed. Veratyrr murdered the May Queen, and the Shadow Court did it to start an attempt to take control of Aeternum They want to kill Evan because once he's dead

Verytyrr will receive the full power of a Court leader. Right now he doesn't have it and the only way to keep it from him is to let Evan live." Evan looked around hopefully. Allana's hands were shaking slightly and he saw her slip them behind her back. Some of the glares had turned contemplative, but more than half of the Court members were still staring at him like a disease.

A Winter Court Fae with grey bird like wings that stretched behind him stood, his hair was white and his eyes were a deep green.

"He is a human, he has crossed into our lands like his ancestors before him, and he has the power of the Shadow Court. No other combination could produce an evil such as this, whether he is behind the May Queen's death or not. He could very well be a part of the Shadow Courts plan to take over."

"I didn't even know this place existed until yest-" *Boom. Shing!* Evan threw his arm over his head and dropped to the ground, pain enveloped his body as shards of glass punctured his arms. *Good thing Allana got me this jerkin.. Allana!* Evan shot upwards and gasped. Over twenty Shadow Court Fae filled the room, dark swords and maces in their hands, grinning and grimacing maliciously.

"A-Allana..." Evan gulped, and his eyes darted back and forth. Hyacinth and most of the other Fae were still on the ground in the fetal position, and the Shadow Court Fae were closing in on him. Flower heavy vines erupted from the floor and wrapped around his waist. "Ahhh! Let go! Bad vines, let go!" He tugged at them, but to no avail. Before he knew it he was flying through the air. He screamed, and a dark haze covered his body. He squeezed his eyes shut. *Like my dream.. Like my grandad...* "Oof!" Evan landed with a hard thump that drove the air from his lungs.

"Shhhhh, I managed to distract them enough to keep their attention from your location, but that won't last long." His eyes shot open. Thea was leaning over him, her eyes were wide with intensity and she had a finger pressed to her lips. As Evan opened his mouth, she glared. Shutting it quickly, he resorted to hand gestures. He pointed at the vines surrounding him and looked at her, eyebrows raised. She nodded, her blue eyes alight with a mischievous glint. Quickly, they crawled between the benches. Bushes covered the entire section so that their path was hidden. Yells filled the air and the ancient sound of battle reigned.

"Flowers? That's what you're going to stop us with. Even for the Spring Court that's pathetic." Thea's eyes narrowed, she turned to Evan.

"I don't know what abilities you have because of your power, but using their own element against them would be a nasty surprise."

"I don't know how to use it. Not on command."

"Well, while you figure that out I'm going to find Allana and show that Shadow Court moron just how pathetic I am." Before Evan could respond Thea vaulted out of the bushes. Evan peeked out from the greenery. A battle unlike any he had ever imagined waged within the courtroom. Winter Fae held swords made of ice and combined sword fighting with a complicated series of what appeared to be Taekwando. They leaped and twisted mid air, their dominant foot landing on the ground while the other flew through the air into their opponent's face, but the Shadow Court operatives were just as skilled and dogged with incredible speed. He spotted Allana wielding double Ice swords against a large Shadow Court Fae, but his size cost him speed and Allana quickly ran him through. He shuddered and looked away as he heard the sickening gasp that erupted from the wounded Fae, and the dull thud that rang out soon after as he slumped to the ground.

A loud yell of rage sounded above all other noise, and Evan caught sight of Thea charging the leader of the Shadow

Court Fae. Her face was red as she sped across the room, staff in hand, and leapt towards him. *Figures, the one time I would actually be useful and I can't pull myself together. This is your chance Evan, to do something worth doing, but no, you have to sit here and hide because you can't figure out how to use your abilities. If only I could make them run, but what could possibly scare them off? Rhere are only forty of them or so, if there were more of us maybe? No that won't work, we already outnumber them slightly. Think, Evan.*

"Don't bother with them, it's the human we want. Find and kill Evan Hale, then the rest of them are as good as dead anyway." Elmer's command rang over the sound of battle.

Me, they're looking for me. How did Elmer do it last night? Would I even be able to? Just do it. Evan burst from the bushes and bellowed.

"Hey over here!!" his voice seemed to echo around him. Ten different Evan's were waving and shouting. Abandoning their fights they stampeded towards the many versions of him including Evan himself. "Oops, gotta run." He bolted from the undergrowth, to his shock and satisfaction the other versions of himself did so as well, all in opposing directions.

Dashing frantically through the open door, Evan glaced around in search of a place to hide. *There's gotta be somewhere here where they won't spot me. Oh my gosh, I can't believe I just did that.* His terrified, exhilarated thoughts were cut off as a figure suddenly rounded the corner in front of him.

"Whoa, relax! It's just me!" Thea whispered as Evan jerked to a halt, hands raised in self-defense. "Come on, we need to get you out of the castle." Too winded to say anything, Evan jogged after her as she rushed back around the corner. "Wow, you sure figured out your power pretty quick," muttered Thea, glancing over her shoulder at Evan. "That was impressive."

"Er, it was still kind of an accident," replied Evan, feeling his face flush.

"Even still," responded the Fae, her eyes on the path ahead. "It should buy everyone some time to escape the castle."

They rounded a corner, Evan sidestepping to avoid crashing into a tree sapling that seemed to be growing out of the floor. "Have you seen Allana?" He asked through each breath.

"No, but I'm sure she's alright." Thea glanced over her shoulder at him. "Come now, surely you know that she can handle herself? She went into your world, after all."

"Our world isn't exactly dangerous. Nobody even knows you guys exist." Evan glanced over his shoulder, relieved to see no sign of anyone following them.

"Well, we thought you might have been the Shadow Court king in disguise," replied Thea. "And, as you can imagine, dealing with such a powerful being who doesn't want to be found comes with a certain amount of danger." She smiled slightly. "Honestly, I had been worried about how long she was taking to report back on her mission, but now that I've seen you in person I can see why she hesitated to believe you're an age- old Shadow Court leader."

"Hey — well, actually, that's fair," Evan chuckled with a smile. "I don't think I'm dark Fae lord material."

Thea opened her mouth to presumably agree before her eyes jerked upward and her body tensed, as though ready to fight.

"What are you —".

Evan turned his head to see a figure lunging from one of the adjacent hallways.

"I've found him! The human is over here!" The cloaked operative made to seize Evan, but a thorny vine from Thea lurched violently from the ground, tossing the attacker down.

Whirling around, Evan could see another soldier rushing toward them, bearing a gleaming sword. He glanced fearfully back at Thea, who was still grappling with their first attacker. *There's no way she'll be able to handle these guys alone!* In desperation, he willed the strange power to come back to him, but the shadow Fae was upon him. The assassin leapt for him, and Evan managed to dive aside. He tried to regain his footing and turn to face his attacker, but an agonizing kick to his side flung him onto the polished stone. Gasping from pain, Evan struggled upright to see the Shadow Court operative looming over him, teeth bared, his sword flashing. He felt something oddly familiar rushing into his arms and, without thinking, jerked out a hand. A sharp jolt bolted through his arm as a jet of darkness leapt from his palm, throwing his attacker backward. The Fae slammed into the wall and crumpled to the ground, unconscious. Panting in exhilaration and exhaustion, Evan looked down at his hands, still surging with the strange, electric feeling. Though there seemed nothing different about them, it felt as though lightning was dancing around just beneath the surface of his skin. *Did I just...?*

Before he could properly take it all in, he heard a gasp from behind him. Whirling around, he saw that the other operative had pinned Thea to the wall. She struggled fruitlessly against his grasp, glancing desperately at her staff lying several feet away. The operative drew back his knife and brought it down.

No! Evan flung out a hand, this time on purpose, and felt the jolting feeling explode from it. In an instant, shadows seized the falling knife, stopping its motion. The operative, his arm frozen in the air by the inky coils, turned his head to face Evan with a dumbfounded look. Instantly, Thea slammed a knee into his stomach, and lunged for her staff. Before the operative could recover from the blow or try to wrench his arm free from the shadows holding it, she brought the end of the staff down hard on his head. The Fae crumpled to the ground, the knife clattering down beside him.

Thea straightened up and peered down at her former assailant, letting her breath out in a long, tense puff as she stared at his unconscious body. "Goodness, I thought I was done for."

"So did I," responded Evan, hands on his knees. The lightning feeling was waning now, as though it had sensed that the danger had passed. "I can't believe I just did that."

"Just in time too." The spring Fae dusted off and met Evan's gaze. "I will remember this. You saved my life."

For a moment, Evan was filled with confusion before remembering that such phrases were the Fae equivalent of "thank you". "Oh, er, okay," he muttered, trying to shrug off the embarrassment making his face grow hot.

Thea glanced around them. "Now come on, we need to get you out of here before more arrive." Gesturing with her staff for Evan to follow, she struck out at a slight jog down the rest of the corridor.

Running to catch up with her, Evan bit back a laugh. "Seriously though, did you see his face when I stopped the sword?"

In spite of the intensity of the situation, Thea grinned. "Utter magnificence. It looked like the type of expression a black bear might make if you tried to convince it to take up figure skating."

The image of Vincent gracefully skating around an ice rink popped into Evan's mind, and he slapped a hand over his own mouth to avoid bursting out laughing.

"You know," muttered Thea, stifling a giggle. "I've heard my whole life about how barbaric and awful humans are, but if they're all kind of like you, I don't see how they're so bad."

* * * * *

Allana was getting dizzy looking for Evan, the battle raged around her and she quickly dispatched her opponent. *He better not do anything stupid. And — too late.*

"Hey over here!!" Evan yelled, Allana groaned. *Just for once couldn't he have stayed put?* but to her astonishment he wasn't the only Evan yellin., Ten others scattered around the room copied the one she saw exactly. *So which one is really him?* Her next opponent stopped mid stroke and rushed towards her friend. Momentarily lost in the chaos, Allana tried to catch a glimpse of each of the Evan duplicates, hoping for some small sign as to which one was real. However, in an instant, they were all out of sight, ducking and weaving out of the room and through the crowd. Pausing to collect herself, Allana glanced around. Many of the shadowy soldiers had dispersed to chase after the Evans, leaving behind the dazed court members. *This might be our only chance to all get out alive.* Rushing up to the top of the stage, she raised her voice above the fearful shrieks and worried mumbling. "Follow me!"

To her shock, the Courts listened, and began to trail after her. She expected the enemy to hound on them. But a quick glance to her surroundings showed that Allanas had joined the Evans as had Court members. In the chaos it would be impossible for the Shadow Court to know which were real. Evan was beginning to lag, a haggard expression on his face. *If Evan is this powerful with just the excess, how much more powerful would Veratyrr himself be?*

Guiding the frightened court members down the wide corridor, Allana rushed toward what she hoped was the quickest exit. She could hear the duplicate court members Evan had instinctively created, shrieking and shouting, as well as the confused yells of the Shadow Court Fae. As they neared the end of the corridor, two figures stepped out in front of them. Allana tensed, her heart leaping into her chest before realizing with a jolt of relief that the figures were Evan and Thea. "Oh, thank goodness," she sighed, rushing forward to meet them. "I was beginning to worry they'd found you."

"They did," responded Thea. "But I'd say we dealt with them alright." She glanced over at Evan who, despite the tense look on his face, gave her a small smile in return.

Seems like she'd warmed up to him a bit, thought Allana. I wonder if there's any chance the courts will follow suit. She opened her mouth to speak, but a volley of shouts from behind her caught her attention. A troop of Shadow Court warriors were sprinting toward her and the court members, led by a Fae with menacing, wasp-like wings. Frantic Fae began pushing and shoving to escape, with a few brave souls standing in the way of the operatives to hold them off.

Allana ran to join the line, squaring up to fight, but a hand on her shoulder stopped her. "Allana, I know you want to help, but someone's got to get Evan out of here," said Thea.

"But—" Allana began before biting her tongue. She's right, I can't just leave Evan alone. After all, it's not like the other court Fae are going to protect him. "Fine," she grunted, watching as Thea nodded and rushed to join the fray. She glanced about, looking for Evan's untidy brown hair amongst the sea of colorful court Fae. "Evan, where'd you go?"

"Here!" A voice behind Allana called. She turned to see Evan squeezing apologetically past a handful of elderly court members who were trying to fight their way to the door. He glanced with ill- disguised terror and worry at the Fae battling to hold the Shadow Court off. "Are we going to help them? They're really outnumbered."

"I wish we could, but we have to get you to—"

A terrified scream echoed out. Allana spun around and gasped. Thea's eyes were wide, and a dark sword was shoved up through her abdomen, red staining her blue bodice. The leader of the Shadow warriors grinned, and slowly the life left her kind, clear, blue eyes. The leader dropped her to the ground. Allana fell to her knees and a scream ripped from her lungs, ringing in her ears. Suddenly, she was a little kid again, a child desperately screaming and fighting against the crushing reality that they were gone, they were never coming back — She felt a hand seize her arm in a tight grip, and heard the broken, shaking voice of Evan shouting for her to get up, to run. She felt herself being tugged upwards, and her own feet beginning to stumble into a run. It all felt so far away, so distant. All she could hear and see was the horrible, gut-wrenching final cry of her friend, and the crimson stains of her friend's blood.

Chapter Eleven

A volley of frantic feet pounded the floor. The shouts of furious Shadow Court Fae and the sounds of battle were fading, but Evan's hand remained tightly clenched unto Allana's. Blind to the acrid smell of burning buildings and scuffling of cowering wildlife, he raced on, dodging waist-high toadstools and curly trees. Allana absently raced on with him, her mind raced with an endless stream of memories, blurring past her in the same manner as the trees. The Shadow Court operative looming over her as she conjured her ice blades, the shrieks of dying Fae, the clash of metal on metal, Thea's body slumping to the ground. Her mind felt numb and yet spun frantically at the same time. *Don't think. Don't think, just run.* Her lungs felt like they might burst from breathing in the filthy air. She was only vaguely aware of the fiery ache in her legs and a nasty cramp developing in her side as she battled with the desperate denial that her friend was gone for good. Her struggle was broken off as several Fae burst from the bushes to their left. Allana skidded to a halt, ice crackling tensely in the palm of her hands as she whirled to face them.

"Don't attack!" yelped a familiar voice. Ember, her face almost unrecognizable under the layer of dust coating her, stepped from the group.

Allana breathed a sigh of relief; her comrades were so filthy from the debris that they almost looked like Shadow Court Fae. She could see the faces of several other members of the Court staff standing among the group, their expressions equally wrought with fear. "Oh, thank goodness, it's just you guys. I thought they'd caught up to us."

"No, the Shadow Court is still stuck at the battlefield. Most everyone was able to escape the castle unharmed." Ember turned to Evan. "Your diversion worked. You saved all of us." Her eyes were much kinder and more welcoming than they had been before.

"Oh, er, of course," gasped Evan, who looked rather shocked to be addressed so gratefully by a Fae.

"Alright, enough chatting," called an agitated voice from the back of the group. An Autumn Court official Allana didn't know by name was glancing about nervously. "The longer we stand here, the more likely we are to be jumped by Shadow Court soldiers. We need to head for the Siege Castle."

Evan opened his mouth as though intending to ask what that was, but closed it a moment after, his brow knit in a grim sort of expression. Allana felt a random stab of pity as the once-curious and question-filled human silently filed after the Fae and couldn't even bother mustering the willpower to express it.

As Allana followed suit, Ember sidled up beside her. "Oh goodness, I'm so worried for my family. Hazel said she saw my mother and father fleeing, so they must be alright, but I can't be too sure, and oh-my poor little fox! I hope he's escaped."

Allana blankly listened to the nervous Fae's fretting, allowing the words to wash over her without bothering to listen to them. She tried to focus on the group ahead of her, her surroundings, anything but the horrible wealth of memories of the battle trying to barge to the front of her mind.

"Oh my goodness, I nearly forgot, have you seen Thea? Daisy's here with the group, but I haven't seen Thea since before the siege started."

Allana's heart seemed to drop to her toes. *Why did you have to ask?* After a moment, she opened her mouth to speak, but the lump in her throat wouldn't permit it. She took in a strangled breath, and finally managed to choke out the words she'd desperately been avoiding saying or thinking. "She's dead."

"What!?" shrieked Ember, clapping a hand over her mouth. "No, there must be some mistake-"

"There's no mistake, Ember," snapped Allana, her voice breaking. "I saw it happen. She's…" Her vision blurred, the tears in her eyes turning the dying sunlight into prisms of red and gold which obscured her vision. Turning away, she quickly strode away from the Queen's Maid, desperate to get away from her shocked stare, and from her tide of questions. Retreating to a spot right behind the group of Fae, Allana took a shaky deep breath, wiping the droplets away from her eyes. Even as she outwardly mastered herself once more, she could feel a painful emptiness in her chest that felt like it might swallow her.

A gentle hand rested on her shoulder. She turned to see Evan meandering beside her. He neither looked at her nor said anything, but his slightly watery eyes were filled with compassion. At the kind gesture of comfort, Allana's grief-wrought heart unclenched a little.

The forest was eerily silent as the small group trekked quietly and quickly along. The beautiful Fae forests that she'd known so well before now seemed menacing and foreign. It was almost as though the Shadow Court had sucked the wonder and liveliness of Aeternum right out. *We should be close to the castle by now, at least I hope. I've only ever heard vague directions about where it's located,* Allana thought. Evan coughed beside her. Glancing over at him, he could see her own tenseness reflected in his face. His glassy eyes were glazed over, as though he were lost in thought. *He must still be thinking about what happened,* she thought. Her heart twisted agonizingly at the very thought of the memory. *Don't think about it, just focus on getting to this castle place safely.*

The bushes parted ahead of them and a figure stepped forward. Frost crackled and wind whooshed as the surrounding Fae tensed for a fight. However, the visitor was anything but a threat. A fairly young and very nervous-looking Summer Court Fae leapt from the bushes, startled at the sight of the group, then breathed a shaky sigh of relief. "Oh, goodness! I thought the sorry few Fae that arrived at the castle were the only ones left." He beckoned frantically to them, glancing about nervously. "Come, follow me. We've been receiving messages that there are Shadow Court Fae making their way into this forest."

While a handful of Fae approached the messenger, most of them lagged behind with distrustful glares. "How do we know you're not one of those Shadow Court Fae, and you're just disguised to lead us into a trap?" barked an older-looking

Fae in the back of the group, who was carrying a small and fearful-looking child. Allana shuddered, remembering how the Shadow operative had disguised himself as a harmless human neighbor to get at Evan. *Please don't let that happen again.*

"Oh!" The Fae quickly fumbled with something hanging around his neck and pulled out what appeared to be some sort of golden seal. Even from afar, Allana could make out the seal of the four Courts upon it. Instantly, a collective sigh rang through the clearing. "Ah, good, good," muttered the messenger, stuffing the seal back within his cloak. "Now, follow me, we've already wasted much time and we don't have much more to spare before they find us." Whirling around, he beckoned the group and trotted silently into the trees.

After what felt like an eternity of tense walking and jumping at any small sound, the trees began to thin, their branches parting to reveal a sky as inky black as the Shadow Court itself. Stepping out from the foliage, Allana found herself gazing upward at the tremendous, moonlit castle of stone, built slightly into the side of an absolutely enormous cliff. She glanced over at Evan, expecting his usual excited gawking, but the boy merely peered up at the castle blankly before following the Fae up the slope. Another pang of sadness pierced her overwrought heart at his bleak indifference. Sighing, she trudged after the small group hastily and clumsily making their way up the steep slope to the castle, stumbling on the loose rocks hiding in the peaty grass.

As they made it up to the large gate, Allana heard the creaking of a bow being drawn. She looked up in alarm to see that a shadowy figure was aiming a crossbow down at the group. *They must be protecting the castle. At least, I hope they are.* "Who's there?" a voice called from above.

"It's Aelius," said the Summer Court messenger who'd been guiding them, brandishing his golden seal once more. "I've come back with more from the castle." A moment passed, then, with a great grinding, the silver gate lifted. Aelius beckoned to them, and they hurried inside the threshold of the castle.

Allana glanced about; they seemed to be in a very plain courtyard of sorts, with a tall, dark wood door at the opposite side. As they approached, Allana could make out the familiar silhouette of Athena standing at the door. *Good, at least she's alright.* As each of the Fae stepped forward to head inside, she carefully took their hand, then nodded them inside with a smile. *She must be checking to make sure they're not disguised Shadow Court Fae,* Allana concluded.

As they stepped up to face the Summer Court Fae, Athena turned. Her face lit up in surprise, and then tremendous relief. "Oh, thank goodness," she sighed, embracing Allana. "I knew those horrible henchmen were after your human friend, and I was worried they might have done something to you because of him." Allana gave her friend a weak , customary smile and opened her mouth to respond.

"You can't *seriously* think of letting them in, can you, Athena?" called a voice dripping with pompousness. Allana whirled around to see Hyacinth, the nasty Spring Court Fae, stepping from the door. He surveyed the on looking Fae and guards with an expression of utmost superiority before his eyes rested on Evan. "This little pestilent creature was the beacon that led the Shadow Court so deep into our lands. You can't just let him in here so that it can happen all over again."

Allana bristled, anger flaring through the numb shock that had settled over her as a thought occurred to her. Hyacinth was just as immaculate as the moment he'd spoken before the Courts, while the surrounding Fae were covered in dust and streaked with blood. *He must've just used his wings and taken off rather than helping the other Fae escape. How can he accuse Athena of endangering the Fae subjects when he abandoned them himself?*

"We discussed this in court," she began, fighting to keep the anger out of her voice, "if we leave him to the Shadow Court, then Verratyr will get a hold of him and obtain the Shadow Heir power, and what happens then? Without a May Queen, we—"

"I didn't ask *you*," spat the Spring Fae, his pale face blushing slightly red. "Goodness knows you're not reliable, you and your love for humans. Be quiet and let the *real* Fae talk about this."

Allana recoiled at the Fae's harsh words, shame and sadness flooding over her. *Of course my opinion doesn't matter, I'm a stupid, human-loving excuse for a Fae. Maybe they'd listen to me more if I treated Evan more like they do.* The thought of spitting such nastiness at Evan twisted her gut. *So I guess that's it then. No matter how hard I try, I'm still useless.*

Evan's voice shocked her out of her thoughts. "Sir," he began evenly, "has Allana ever *actually* given you reason to think that she isn't a reliable Fae? For heaven's sake, she served under your Queen, and risked going into our world to find her assassin when she was killed. Why would she do that if she wasn't reliable and willing to do anything for her kingdom?" He met the shocked gaze of the regal Fae firmly, though Allana could see his hands shaking slightly.

Allana gawked at Evan, her mouth slightly open in shock. *He's willing to stand up against someone like Hyacinth to help me?*

Hyacinth seemed to finally regain his composure. "Don't talk about things you don't understand, *human*," he said, glaring down his nose at him. His glistening wings rose in a menacing sort of way, as though trying to frighten him. Evan straightened up taller, firmly glaring back at his adversary, one hand gently grasping his bullet necklace.

Before either of them could speak, Athena stepped forward. "Hyacinth, who was raised by whom doesn't matter right now. What matters is that if the Shadow Court gets ahold of the human and his power, we'll be in much deeper water. This castle is also built to survive brutal assaults, so why shouldn't the human stay?" Before Hyacinth could open his mouth once more, Athena ushered Allana and Evan inside.

* * * * *

The next few minutes seemed to go by in such a blur that Evan could hardly pay attention to them. When they arrived inside, someone immediately directed them to where they would be staying. Following a Fae as they navigated the large, empty corridors of the castle, Evan found herself standing in front of a tiny bedroom with two rickety-looking beds inside. Sauntering past Evan, Allana slumped fully dressed onto the nearest bed. Evan felt as though every bone in his body weighed several tons, and dragged himself across the dusty stone floor to his own bed. Yanking off his shoes, he flopped backwards onto the covers. For a few agonizing moments, he fought off the torrent of horrid memories from the passing day trying to fight their way to the surface of his mind. However, his physical exhaustion overpowered his mental agony, and soon he felt sleep gently pulling him off. He let the comforting embrace take him far away from the tragic memories and destruction of the previous day, from his worries about what would happen.

Suddenly, he was slammed into cold, damp stone. He struggled to stand, but a booted foot slammed him to the ground once more with such force that it drove the breath from his lungs.

"That — that was much easier — Than I thought it would be," gasped a voice. It was out of breath, yet icy cold and full of such malignant triumph that it made Evan's blood feel as though it might freeze. He looked up to see a young man standing over him. He brushed a strand of ebony hair away from his unnerving green eyes that glittered like venomous snake scales, and a cruel smirk crossed his face. His hand moved, and Evan looked down to see him fingering a gruesome jet-black blade that gleamed evilly in the dim light of the large, echoey cavern they seemed to be standing in.

Evan's mouth began to move of its own accord. "What do you think killing me will accomplish? Your plot will be found out before you can so much as return to the castle, Verratyr," he choked out. Despite the intensity of the conversation, Evan was distracted by an odd draining, pulsing feeling, as though something was trying to pull him beneath nonexistent waters. Glancing down toward what felt like the source of the throbbing, he saw a small rip in his regal clothing, with a small, shallow cut in the skin beneath. His attention was diverted from the wound as Verratyr took one menacing step closer, drawing himself up with pride. As he fearfully met the gaze of his assailant, the pulse of his Shadow power surged down his arm and throbbed in his palm as it slowly built up.

Verratyr snorted mirthlessly. "I knew you were foolish, but I didn't know you were this stupid. Who do you think will find you, down here in this damp hole? Your royal subjects most certainly won't. They're too caught up in their pitiful, mundane lives to care about searching for a ruler that would never do the same for them."

"You say that as if you would," Evan snapped back fiercely. "You couldn't care less about — " A kick from Verratyr struck him hard in the chin, and his head was once again flung back into the stone. Flashes of light like stars burst into his vision, and the irony taste of blood filled his mouth.

Through his slitted eyelids, he could see Verratyr fingering the handle of the enchanted knife, looking cold and unconcerned. "All of your advisors and officials have been discussing how much more they prefer me on the Shadow Court throne, so I find it highly unlikely they'll come looking for a king they no longer desire." He smirked.

Evan gave an odd gasp of surprise, and experienced an unexplained feeling of betrayal. "You're lying," he snarled, his mouth once again moving outside of his volition. "You know as well as I that my people would never want the bloodshed you will bring upon them." He made a feeble attempt to stand, resting a hand against a nearby stone and trying valiantly to force his legs up. He lunged weakly at Veratyrr, but with no strength left in him, the Shadow Court Fae merely sidestepped. Evan slumped with an agonized grunt to the ground, hauling himself around to face his attacker.

"Oh, how pathetic," crooned Verratyr's voice cruelly from behind. "Poor king Tablarye, weak inside and out, so filled with the delusion that he is a great leader. I might as well just end it now," Evan turned to see the Fae standing over him. He had spread his eerily inky black wings, blotting out the dim light shining from the exit above. His eyes were cold, hateful, and merciless, and his mouth was twisted in a grimace of disgust as he glared down at Evan. Suddenly, Evan shot out his concealed hand, and the feeling of energy across his palm jolted forth like a bolt of lightning. What almost looked like a creature constructed purely of shadows lunged at Verratyr. The knife went spinning out of his hand as he was flung to the ground. "Agh!" Evan lunged, but it was not for the nearby knife. He leapt into the air, and suddenly he was flying, heading toward the light. Searing pain was rapidly building from the small cut on his arm, half- blinding them as it sapped his remaining

strength. He could hear Verratyr shrieking furiously after him, then –

Jolting upright with a gasp, Evan glanced frantically about. Moonlight was casting a dim luminosity across a small and familiar room. *Oh, thank goodness, it was just a dream.* He felt the spot where the gruesome slash had been inflicted upon him by the knife. *Why did it feel so real then? That pain was real, really real. Wait – Wasn't Verratyr that guy that Allana brought up?* Flopping back against his pillow, Evan stared up at the slightly cracked ceiling, tying to sort out the mess of questions in his head. *This has happened twice now. First that strange dream about grandad, and now this. I dunno, maybe these kinds of weird dreams are normal in Aeternum.*

As he lay there, an odd thought occurred to him. The memory of using his shadow power to escape Veratyrr in the dream stuck particularly strongly. He thought of how he had coaxed it to come from his hands, and the adrenaline-filled memory of what he'd done during the siege on the castle returned to him. Lifting a hand, he focused on willing the odd feeling to come. Moments passed, and nothing happened. Suddenly, a small flicker of the jolting feeling danced through his arm, and he felt a thrill of excitement. *I think I've got it!* Slowly, the feeling grew, and before he knew it, Evan was holding a little black shadow in his hand. It wreathed around his fingers, and Evan watched it in shocked wonder. *This is amazing.*

* * * * *

Allana turned over again, sighing wearily. Hours had gone by, yet sleep continued to evade her. *Why must my body try to torture itself? Every part of me has been aching for sleep, yet the moment I lie down, I can't.* Tossing and turning once more, Allana brushed away several flakes of ice that had formed on her palms in annoyance. A gasp caught her attention. Sitting up slightly, she saw Evan watching a little shadow dancing about in the palm of his hand with an expression of utmost awe. "What are you doing?" She croaked. Evan jerked around to face the voice, the Shadow disappearing in a little puff.

"Oh, er, nothing," said Evan, unconvincingly.

"Suure. Don't mess around with that power, goodness knows what it can do," muttered Allana, adjusting her pillow. "I'm guessing I'm not the only one finding it hard to sleep, then."

"Hey, every other time I've used it I either saved my own skin or someone else's, so I'd say I know what it can do. And it's not that I'm having a hard time sleeping, I'm just having weird dreams." Evan rubbed the back of his neck, looking deep in thought. Finally, he looked up. "Er, this sounds kind of strange, but is it normal to have weird, vivid dreams in Aeternum? I just dreamt that the Verratyr guy you mentioned before was trying to murder me with this weird black sword. And a little while ago I had this other dream where I saw something from a story my grandfather had told me, except it was really vivid and real."

As Evan lapsed into thoughtful silence, Allana swallowed her mild shock. *Wait, black sword? How would he know about the enchanted black weapons the Shadow Court possess?* Suddenly, it hit her. *Oh, of course.* She turned to Evan. "I think you must be experiencing the memories of past possessors of the Shadow Heir power. That kind of thing happened with the May Queen too. Sometimes, she'd tell me about some of the odd nightmares she'd get of past wars and battles that the former May Queen had fought." She trailed off, trying to ignore the painful stab in her heart at the memory of her friend's contemplative face as she shared those interesting tales. Pulling herself from her reverie, she saw Evan watching her with a sympathetic expression, and felt a mild stab of annoyance. *I don't need your pity, thank you.*

"Huh, interesting," responded Evan. He paused, rubbing a scrape on his arm that he'd undoubtedly received during the building collapse. Finally, he looked up, looking tentative as he spoke. "Did you know the May Queen well? You kind of talk about her like you do."

Allana hesitated. *He's a stupid human,* she tried to tell herself, *he wouldn't understand.* But something about the look in the boy's eyes, especially when he mentioned his grandfather. It was subtle, but she realized there was a worn look that only came with the grief of death that was always lingering in the depths of his eyes. Those depths seemed to say he might understand more than she thought, and certainly more than any Fae in all of Aeternum. Finally, she relented. "Yes," she sighed, "she and Thea were the only Fae who didn't think I was some sort of weird, intelligence lacking abomination, because I was raised b-by humans." Allana looked down. "I didn't come to Aeternum till I was seven. I never saw my human family again, and never really had a family again either." She sighed bitterly.

"You were raised by humans?" Evan was incredulous. "What were they like? Did you have any siblings?" Excitement was infused in his voice and he bounced slightly on his mattress. Allana let out a short laugh.

"Ha, yeah, I was raised by humans, and yes I had an older brother, Jay, h-he uh, died in a car crash the day I was taken here. I never got to say goodbye. You remind me of him sometimes." A tear slid off the edge of her eye; silently she reached up and brushed it away.

Evan's face was still wreathed with shock, and understanding flooded his eyes. Allana turned away and hugged her pillow tightly."Why did she let him win, and let that happen?" Allana muttered

"Let what happen?" asked Evan. Allana jumped; she didn't think he had been able to hear her

"Nothing," she grumbled.

"Oh, come on!" said Evan, a spark of his former liveliness appearing once more as he glared over her with a half-frustrated, half-amused expression. "You can't act all sarcastic when I pull the 'nothing' card and then pull it yourself."

Allana scowled over at him. Part of her didn't want to express the question that had been burning agonizingly in her mind since the May Queen's demise because of how painful it still was to think over, but another part of her thought that if she kept anything else clogged up within her mind, she might actually explode. She took a breath in, the words tumbling out of her mouth. "The May Queen is the most powerful being in our world and by extension the human world as well, by far. Even the most powerful Shadow Court Fae wouldn't stand a chance normally, even with enchanted weaponry. I want to know why she died, why she *let* herself die, when she would have defeated Veratyrr easily." Allana lapsed into silence, glaring down at the tiny shards of frost beginning to creep across her hands. A silence stretched across the room, and Allana wondered if Evan had even understood what she said.

Finally, Evan spoke. He spoke slowly, as though he were carefully considering each word. "I thought the same thing when my grandfather died. He had cancer, and the doctors said that, even though it would take a long time and be very difficult for everyone, they might be able to treat it. But my grandfather told them no." His voice had grown quiet, and it shook with pent up emotion, he was staring unseeingly at the opposite wall. "We begged him to let them try, but he didn't want to. He said he didn't think it was worth it. I couldn't understand why he'd do that, why he'd just leave us like that when there was a chance he could've lived." He paused, looking reflective. "Maybe they both decided to let those things happen. Maybe they knew something we didn't."

"Maybe," mumbled Allana. An odd feeling of comfort had washed over her. *It's nice to have someone who understands how I feel, who doesn't ignore me or scoff.* For a moment, the fact that Evan was a human seemed to slip from her mind, and she felt grateful for his company. She snapped out of her thoughts. "Well, I'm glad you shared that." When silence met her words, she glanced up. Evan was looking oddly at her, his head slightly cocked to the side, as though he'd just noticed something about her. "What?" she asked crossly.

Evan shook his head. "Oh, nothing." Realizing his mistake, he looked up with an apologetic grin.

Allana snorted, trying and failing to hold back a smile. "Oh, come on, are we really back to that?"

"Shut up," Evan grinned, and then a silent signal seemed to pass between them and they both layed back down. The comfort of knowing an understanding friend was near, blanketed the room and seemed to protect and quiet their minds as sleep overtook them.

Morning dawned all too quickly for Evan's liking. He groaned as he sheltered his newly opened eyes from the sunlight pouring in through the window. Just as he was hauling himself upright, he felt a wad of fabric smack him on the side of his head. "Wha —?"

"C'mon, go get changed. We need to concoct some sort of plan," Allana's bossy voice called to him.

Evan yanked the shirt that had flopped over his eyes. The clothing for the most part looked the same as what he had been wearing, except it was devoid of the thick layer of dust and grime it had accumulated during the previous day's events. He glanced up at Allana, rubbing an eye blurred by sleep. "How long have you been up?"

"Not important. Now, hurry up!" She smirked slightly at his groggy countenance before rushing away in a flurry.

Moaning, Evan hauled himself out of the rickety bed and dragged his feet toward the restroom. By the time he returned, he found Allana shoving several apples into a tattered- looking rucksack. "So, what's the plan?" he asked.

Allana paused from her packing. "So, I've spoken to Athena and several other Court members this morning, and we agreed the only way Aeternum can truly be safe again is if Verratyr is killed," she began. *Gosh, someone got an early start to the morning,* thought Evan. "They agreed that your power will be vital. See, your Shadow Court power should allow you to be able to track the location of the Shadow Court, which no non-Shadow Court Fae can do."

"But how do I—"

"Which should allow us to get to Veratyrr," continued Allana, as though she hadn't heard him. "Athena said she'd speak to the other Court members about how that'll happen, and who we should bring with us."

Almost on cue, the door swung open, and Athena stepped into the room. Her face was slightly flushed, and Evan could see her fists clenched. *Yikes, I'm guessing something didn't go well.* "Bad news, Allana," she growled, walking up to them. "*Hyacinth* stepped in on the issue. He seemed to think it was useless wasting a well-trained fighter on the mission that could either return Fae to normal or end it." She breathed out heavily, her brow furrowed in anger. "I wish I could do something about it, but he's a higher ranking official than I am, and has most of the other pompous fools convinced that we shouldn't bother with 'silly pointless suicide missions'." She turned to Evan, looking apologetic. "I'm sorry to say, but this is probably because you spoke up against him . He was ranting all evening about 'the nerve of that human creature', and I have a feeling he wanted to punish you for speaking against him."

Evan heard the faint crackling of ice in Allana's palms as she bristled and gritted her teeth. "So he'd risk the whole Fae world just so he could 'punish' me?"

"Not entirely," said Athena, looking as though she'd like to be doing anything else than defending Hyacinth. "I just don't think he fully believes the allegations against Verratyr and is scared to act in any way that could possibly jeopardize the Courts further."

"So what do we do now?" snarled Allana, starting to pace. "Take him on ourselves?"

"I really don't know," responded Athena. "I could try pleading to the others once more, but they seem equally set in their ways, and I don't know if we even have that kind of time. There have already been sightings of Shadow Court operatives very close to this castle and, while we might be able to hold out for quite a while, it will only be a matter of time before they take this castle too.."

"Well, what if we just go by ourselves then?" blurted Evan. As the two Fae turned to him with expressions of confusion, he backtracked. "Okay, hear me out. We need to act immediately, and since we don't have anyone who can accompany us, we need to go ourselves. Plus, they wouldn't see it coming."

Allana gawked at Evan as though he'd suggested something absolutely insane, but Athena looked thoughtful. "That actually might work. After all, you would have the advantage because Evan has the Shadow Heir power, which technically makes him stronger than Veratyrr. And Allana, as a Queen's Maid, you were trained so that you could protect him if need be." She paused, meeting Allana's gaze. "And really, it might be the only thing you can do."

Allana's gaze danced between the two of them, her brow scrunched as she thought on the decision. After a moment, she sighed, and straightened up. "Fine, we'll sneak out the back entrance and leave at once.

Chapter Twelve

While their mission had started out filled with determination and fervor, Evan could feel his own dwindling. His feet were beginning to ache from picking his way over rough, uneven ground coated in patchy layers of slippery pine needles, and the slight warmth that had been rather pleasant when they had first set off was now creating uncomfortable beads of sweat across his face. *Gosh, now would be a good time to have some of those wings the special Fae have.*

"How far along are we?" Allana asked. Evan furrowed his brow in concentration.

Though Athena had taken a few minutes to explain to Evan how exactly to read his ability to detect the Shadow Court based off of her own powers, he still wasn't very confident. Furrowing his brow in concentration and worry, he squinted against the sunlight blaring in past the sparse cover of young pine trees. "I think we're getting closer. I kind of lost concentration a while back…"

"You *what*?" exclaimed Allana, panic and agitation flaring across her face "Why didn't you tell me? We could be wildly off course right now!"

"Yeah, I know, I know," grumbled Evan, "but I'm pretty sure I have it figured out, and I don't think you would have been able to help anyway." *I'm the one who's never had magic training before and has to track something I don't understand. You just have to walk behind me. So get off my back about it.* Evan thought irritatedly, it had gotten hotter as they traveled, and the constant use of concentration to sense the Shadow Court lands was tiring him further. Evan saw Allana open her mouth to retort but closed it again. Shifting her rucksack she plodded on with him. Evan was grateful she didn't push the issue further. After several long minutes of silence, an odd thundering met Evan's ears. He glanced around, aware that Allana was doing the same. *What is* – his thoughts were cut off as a blur of white and silver shot from the trees to their left. For a moment, images of the Shadow Court henchmen chasing after them burst into mind, and he prepared to fight, then he noticed shining horns coming off of the horde's forehead. *Your kidding, it can't be..*

"Unicorns!" Gawking in excitement, Evan grinned ear to ear as the elegant, horse- like creatures came to a halt in a patch of undergrowth about twenty feet away from them, dropping their muzzles into the greenery to graze. Behind him he heard Allana sigh weakly in relief. "Alright, we need to—" Evan knew that Allana was speaking but he was too caught up with the fact that unicorns were real, to pay attention. Evan reached out a hand to a curious unicorn. "Hi," he muttered gently to the creature, who gingerly bumped its soft nose against his fingers with an expression of hesitant curiosity.

"Evan, for heavens' sake! Quit making friends and come on!" barked Allana. The unicorn, at the sudden loud noise, spun around in fear and bolted back to its herd.

Whirling around, Evan glared at Allana. "Why'd you do that?" he asked. *She's always such a jerk!*

"We don't have time to look at nature," retorted Allana, balling her hands into fists. "In case you haven't noticed, the fate of Aeternum rests on our shoulders! We need to focus!"

Evan glared angrily at her for several moments before finally letting out a tense sigh. "Fine." Walking past her, he continued into the forest.

I have to be going the right way, right? Thought Evan with a rising sense of panic that even the image of the unicorns couldn't stifle. He tried to concentrate on the odd, clammy sensation Athena had pointed out as his Shadow

Court power directing him to its homeland. It felt stronger than when they'd first started out, but had recently seemed to flatline in its strength. *Maybe if I just turn and walk a little in a random direction, I'll be able to gauge where I am. Kind of like a weird, magical compass.* Taking a sharp turn, Evan headed toward a slight downhill slope covered in a thick padding of moist pine needles. As his foot hit the slant, he felt himself slide and, flailing about furiously, managed to snag a nearby pine branch for support. He heard a snicker from Allana and, instead of the usual laugh that often bubbled in his throat at his friend's amusement, he felt an odd stab of anger and annoyance. Shaking it away halfheartedly, he continued to slip and slide down the slope, Allana following suit. As he gratefully stumbled onto even ground, he was suddenly aware of feeling slightly warmer than before. *Did the weather change over here…? Oh no, it's because that weird clammy feeling has lessened. I went in the complete opposite direction!*

"What?" asked Allana. "You look like you've just— oh, we went the wrong way, didn't we?"

"Er, yes," muttered Evan. Not wanting to see the Fae's expression of incredulity at his "pitiful human mistake," Evan whirled around and wordlessly began scrabbling back up the slippery hill. He heard an equally annoyed and begrudging sigh from behind him, and the scrape of pine needles and crackling of frost as Allana followed suit.

Several long minutes later, and Evan mercifully became aware of the feeling growing once more. *Finally, we're back on track.* He glanced up at the sky, wishing the sun would move across the sky quicker so that it would finally cool off. Though it wasn't very hot, the effort it took to saunter over the spongy, rough earth made it feel as though they were hiking through the desert. Looking back down, Evan saw a steep, rocky uphill that stretched out of sight. *Oh great, will we have to climb that?*

Allana answered his unspoken question. "We'll waste daylight if we try to find a way around. We'll just have to go over it." Without waiting for Evan's response, she trotted up to the rocky uphill and began slowly picking her way up it, using her hands to stabilize herself when it got steeper.

Taking a deep breath and adjusting his rucksack, Evan took his first step onto the rocks. Instantly, he felt his shoes, still slick from the pine needles, begin to slide. Grasping at any exposed root or grippy rock he could see, he hauled himself up after Allana. The Fae was having much better success than he was, and was steadily leaving him behind. "Allana, wait—" his voice was cut off as the motion of leaning up to yell to Allana caused one of his feet to slip. Gritting his teeth against a yelp of pain as his knee slammed against the rock face, he frantically reached for a nearby ledge. *I feel like I'm gonna slide backwards down the whole thing!* He glanced up to where Allana was.

The Fae had just reached the top, and seemed to have only just realized the trouble her companion was in. She gawked irritably down at him. "What are you— nevermind, I'm coming." Slipping and sliding back down to Evan, she offered a hand to him, which he gratefully took, and soon the two had managed to scale the rest of the slippery hill.

As they reached the top, Evan turned to Allana. Perhaps it was the scrapes and bruises from the slip on his arms and knee or the heat, but he found himself feeling irrationally angry. "Why didn't you respond to me the first time?" he asked, trying to keep the snippiness from his voice. "It wasn't like I was too far away for you to hear me."

"Hey, I was trying to focus on climbing," retorted Allana defensively, "I didn't have concentration to spare on babysitting you."

Anger flared sharply in Evan's chest, and he felt his face flush. "There's a difference between *babysitting* someone and the basic kindness of helping someone, you know," he snapped. Allana's mouth lolled open slightly, as though taken aback at his snippy retort, and Evan, feeling shocked and awkward about the outburst himself, hurriedly dusted off his pants and meandered onward. The tense sound of fast footfalls alerted him of Allana catching up, and an uncomfortable silence ensued.

They kept walking. It felt like hours had passed before they finally made it to the end of the thin pine forest. Evan stayed behind her. He felt like this might be better. After all, they were both still very mad at each other. He thought he had a right to be mad. She *did* basically try to kill him in the first place if he thought about it. He knew Allana cared, but he felt like something was holding her back from actually expressing it. Maybe she didn't care. He couldn't tell anymore. As sweat dripped down his forehead, he felt his shirt on his sweaty back pull away as a breeze hit them hard in the face. Even though it was hot, he shivered.

They came once again to another forest of pine trees, though this one wove together much more thickly than the last. Allana looked hesitant to step into this forest so he stepped into it first. He made an 'after you' gesture, and Allana gave him a weird look before leading him into the forest.

As they stepped into it, Evan was suddenly aware of a temperature drop. *Wow, it makes quite the difference to just be in the shade here,* he thought. After a few minutes of walking, he noticed there was no more sun although it was nowhere near sunset. He looked up to see trees crossing each other, blocking out any sunlight and making sure only darkness was there. He looked around, very cautious, then kept walking. For some reason, he felt as if a pair of eyes had been watching them walk. His throat was parched but he didn't dare ask Allana for the water because something in him told him that she might get angry. He decided to stay thirsty.

They kept walking. A sound came from a bush and they both stopped. Evan got behind Allana, who was in front of the bush. Allana pointed her hands at it, evidently to shield them with her power if need be. Several tense moments passed before their fear at the possible threat faded.

"Must have been some little jungle creature," muttered Allana tensely. "C'mon, the power was leading you this way, right?"

"Yeah," replied Evan, relaxing slightly. He turned to follow Allana when a blur of motion next to him made him jump out of his skin. As something small hopped out of the bush at them, Evan let out a long, high pitched squeal like scream before noticing it was a small bunny. He felt his face turn red as Allana looked back at him and rolled her eyes then started to walk away. He looked at the bunny, smiled and then frowned, noticing that this so called bunny had four eyes and it had purple fur. Though all of the other critters he'd come across in Fae had given off a sense of friendly companionship, this one left him with an odd, uncomfortable feeling. "W-wait up, Allana!" He yelled, running towards her, faster.

As he looked around, Evan felt as if someone was staring at them. He wouldn't be surprised. After all, he had just screamed. Evan could tell Allana was irritated at him for doing that, for the past hour neither of them had said a word to each other. There had been a moment when he had thought she was going to talk to him and apologize but she saw him looking at her and had immediately stiffened up and stalked off. *It's like she thinks if she apologizes she's losing or something. Which is ludicrous, but she's always cold like this so I don't know why I'm even surprised, he* contemplated bitterly. He thought he saw something move in the bushes; Allana did too because she started looking around, hands outstretched, ready to freeze anything that came close. After a tense couple of minutes they kept walking. Suddenly a dark blurry form appeared right behind his friend. He called out to her."Allana!"

Evan's alarmed voice brought Allana to a halt, and she turned around. The figure leaped at her and they toppled to the floor. Evan was dumbstruck. He didn't know what to do; if he shot Shadow at them he would hit Allana too, and he had no idea what affects his powers actually had on people. Worriedly he waited for an opening and watched. A jet of ice burt from Allana's fingertips and flew toward the operative's face, and he deflected it quickly with a blast of dark, shadowy material, but the temporary distraction allowed Allana to leap to her feet. Rapidly creating a roughly hewn ice dagger, she turned to see the Fae lunging for her once more. She sidestepped, swinging her dagger down to plunge into his shoulder, but the operative swooped out of the way just in time. The operative lunged again, and Allana leapt out of the way, making another attempt to slash him with her ice blade.

Evan rushed forward to help his friend but when he got close, she stood up and he was afraid that he would get in her way.

This time, her blow hit home, catching her assailant on the side. However, the rough edges of the blade snagged on the thick fabric, and she was jerked off balance. *Wham!* A fist slammed hard into the slide of her face, and she was flung sideways into a tree. Evan gasped and rushed their assailant. Allana was stumbling around, her vision obviously hindered. But he didn't get there in time, the dark Fae slashed his friend's leg with his blade and Allana cried out in anguish, falling to the ground with a thump. The Shadow Fae loomed over her. "Allana!" He jumped on top and tackled the person and then slammed them against a tree. Something came out of this person's mouth, a hiss-like whimper. He looked at Allana on the ground, eyes closed, blood all over her pants. He let his grip loosen on the attacker and scrambled to Allana. Theattacker ran in the opposite direction. He got up to chase them but then decided he needed to attend to Allana. He watched as they went flying away, hissing and whimpering probably from an injury Evan just gave them when they'd hit the tree. He shook Allana, waiting for an answer. "Allana. Allana! Wake up. Please wake up." He reached up and placed two fingers on her neck, checking for a pulse like his father taught him to do. He noticed she was breathing in and out still.

His vision went a bit blurry, but he blinked the feeling away. He then saw her leg, swollen and covered with red. With shaking hands, he ripped his sleeve and placed it on her leg then tightened it. She whimpered.

"Sorry, I have to put some sort of bandage on it," he muttered quietly. Her eyes flickered open, and he saw tears of pain cloud her ghostly irises. Evan took a deep breath then looked down at her neck. The deep red marks left by the attacker's fingernails had begun to swell angrily. He then got up, grabbed the water bottle and poured some onto her leg and let her take it from him. She could barely hold it up on her own. He thought maybe she had a concussion, there was certainly blood on her temple and she definitely needed to rest. He grabbed a huge leaf that swung low to the ground from a tree above and yanked it. He placed it over Allana and got some wood and sticks from the ground. He gathered them up and grabbed the matches they'd snagged before leaving, lighting the pile of wood. Soon, a small, crackling fire was dancing merrily before them.

He looked back at Allana, her breathing was deep, and her mouth hung open slightly due to her slacked jaw. *She fell asleep fast. At least her breathing is deep and not shallow. Wait, isn't it bad for concussed people to sleep right after the injury? No, she got injured and she should rest.* Evan tried to stifle his worry, there was no way she had anything less than a concussion, and now that Allana was asleep he was doubting whether he should have let her or not. He sat down by the crackling fire. He needed to keep watch. No way he would let anyone hurt them again. Not like this. He felt his eyes get heavy and laid his head on his knees which were between his arms. He could feel himself drifting off to sleep, he shook his head violently and forced himself to lift his head, trying his best to stay awake. The sound of the fire made him miss his home, his bed, his family. He wanted to give up right there and then and go home but could he? Would this world end if he ran away and went back home to his parents and Noel? He missed his job and Vincent. He missed everything. *I can't turn back now though. Not now that so much is at stake.*

Evan could hear Allana shivering, his heart sank, it hadn't been under eighty degrees in days. *She must have an infection, but I don't have anything that can help her.* Looking over at her he saw her attempt to get up but within seconds she gave up and laid back down, a sigh of despair escaping her lips. He heard a small sniff. He glanced at her again and saw silent tears running down her feverish cheeks. He rushed over to her. "Allana! What — what's wrong?"

"I don't know. I just never seem to know anymore." She took a deep breath in and out and wiped away her tears. Evan scooted closer towards her. If he were to do that a few days ago, she would not have let it happen but now, *She's probably too tired to stop me.* "Sorry, Evan. I didn't mean to —"

"No. It's okay. Trust me."

He knew the urge to give up must be stronger with her, with how banged up she was. It was hard enough for him to go on and he only had a few scrapes and bruises. They both wanted to give up. Allana lifted her leg and breathed harsh air from her lungs. Evan rushed to help her get to her feet.

"We should keep walking. I've held us up long enough." Evan nodded mutely, usually he would contradict the self deprecating phrasing, but she wasn't wrong and he was too tired to come up with half truths. As they walked, Evan could see his friend grit her teeth in pain as she favored her injured leg.

"We can re-" Evan began, trying to suggest they take a longer rest, but she cut him off.

"I appreciate it, really, and I'm sorry I've been so irritable. But we can't waste any more time; the longer we wait the more likely it is we'll be found." She tried to smile at him. Evan appreciated the gesture and smiled back. Together they hobbled on.

He followed Allana. He felt bad for her. She was injured, seriously. He was grateful to her for apologizing. It seemed to clear some of the tension. He could tell she really did mean it. She must have felt bad but she shouldn't feel bad. She was so hurt that he felt bad. Her leg was all red, her neck the same. He couldn't imagine how it felt to see your life flash before your eyes as someone choked you almost to death. He wondered what she was thinking when that happened. He knew that they needed to rest. Allana needed to rest, for sure. She was limping but she still kept on moving. He looked around, very cautious. He couldn't let anything like that happen again, especially not to Allana. Her body couldn't take another hit. After what seemed like hours, they stopped. Well, at least Evan stopped. He called to Allana. She came back to the little cave where he was standing.

"Look, Allana. We should rest here. I'll check inside to make sure it's safe for us and then I'll look for some food. Alright?" Allana nodded her head. He grabbed a match from his back pocket and put it in front of him. He was a little hesitant to go into this random cave but they had no time to be scared. He waved his lighter and went in. He looked around to see sticks strewn throughout the cave and nothing else. He walked back out. "It's safe. Go ahead and rest in there and I'll look for wood for a fire."

"Okay."

He stepped out as Allana limped into the cave. He looked around outside and found tiny branches scattered across the ground which he picked up. After getting about thirty of them, he went into the cave and put them in a pile near the sleeping Allana. He lit them with his lighter as they burst into a fire. He then stepped out again.

After looking around for about thirty minutes, Evan stopped by a bush and spotted the slight gleam of berries. He went camping all the time with his dad when he was younger so he knew which berries were poisonous and which weren't. *Except that was back in the human world. Here, I don't have any idea.* He felt himself reminiscing about when his dad taught him how to survive and he wondered if they were worried, which they probably were. He had disappeared out of nowhere. Luckily, as he got closer he saw that they were the same silver berries Allana had picked from a bush and handed to him before. *That feels like eons ago.* He picked them and ate one. It tasted delicious. He picked about forty and started walking back to where the cave was. He looked around, always cautious, making sure no one was following him.

He observed all around him. Tiny bugs crawled up a tree. The bugs had neon stripes on them which made them interesting to look at. After stopping to look at these bugs, he decided he needed to get food to Allana. He remembered that she was in pain so he needed to get to her as soon as possible. He finally reached the cave and went in. The fire was crackling as he shook Allana to wake her. She turned over to look at Evan. He poured about half of the pile of berries in her hand and she sat up to eat them. She looked very hungry as she popped one into her mouth. He then sat beside her and dug out some of the other food they'd brought with them, distributing it between them.

After they'd finished their meal, Evan settled down as comfortably as he could on the hard rock floor. He noticed Allana had already fallen asleep in that short time. She must've been so tired from all the walking she was doing with her leg. He looked at the fire. He felt a wave of hopelessness wash over him. He wanted to go back. He wondered if Allana felt the same way. *I know we can't though, we both do. But there has to be some hope that we can make it, right?*

He kept the rucksack around his torso and laid down, too tired to take it off. He put his hands under his head. He found himself thinking about Vincent and how he was doing. Hopefully he was doing okay. He missed sharing his leftovers. Once he went to that park again, he definitely had to see Vincent and tell him all about what he discovered, about the journey he took. He couldn't wait to hug his parents again and talk to them. He couldn't wait to see Noel again and take her out for ice cream everyday like he used to over the summer, before all of this happened. He just needed to complete this journey, if that's what he would call it. He couldn't wait to get back to his job and see all of the little pets. He did really miss everything. The thought of leaving Aeternum, Allana and the beautiful world he'd discovered didn't sit well with him though, despite all of the pain and suffering that had transpired. *Maybe they'll still let me visit*, he thought hopefully. He felt his thoughts drifting away into drowsiness. He needed to sleep. He felt his eyes close and everything went black.

The back of Evan's neck prickled, like a slow bead of hot sweat was trickling all the way down his spine. He shot up, feeling his neck with his hand. There was no sweat. He looked outside the cave and clapped his hand to his mouth to stop himself from gasping. Less than ten feet away stood four pairs of black boots, and harsh voices talked outside of the cave opening.

"Sadly, Lord Veratyrr wants the pleasure of killing them himself; we can injure them as much as necessary as long as we don't kill them ourselves."

Evan shook with fear, scrambling farther into the cave, he nudged Allana. Whispering as quietly as he could into her ear.

"A-Allana," he croaked, Shock had a hold on him causing a stutter.

"What?" she said non too quietly.

"Shh! The shadow guys are right outside, in front of the cave entrance. We gotta get past them somehow."

"Evan, I can barely see straight. How am I supposed to help get past them?" Allana's voice was fueled with irritation. Evan looked fearfully at the cave opening. The black boots were getting closer until the threatening Fae were easily seen within their hiding place.   Evan couldn't think straight, before he knew it one had grabbed him by the arm. He tried to get away, but he was leaning against the cave wall, and escape was impossible. *Come on Shadow power, I could really use you right now.* Evan pleaded with his Fae Alter Ego, trying desperately to summon a power he didn't understand.

"Move it, welp," the attacker commanded. *Well, I can't really fight him, so I might as well make his job harder.* So Evan jutted his chin out and flopped limply to the floor, his wrist still encapsulated by his enemy. He could almost hear Allana rolling her eyes at him, but he didn't care. It was four against two, what could he do? *More like one and a half, considering Allana's physical state, h*e thought grimly. The guard sighed above him, and slowly began to drag Evan across the cave floor and into the open. *Well that sure worked well.*

"Ow."

"Cold!" Two voices rang out in succession. The Fae dragging Evan paused for a moment. The sound of racing feet disappearing in the distance.

"It doesn't matter, the boy is who Lord Verratyr wants, and, injured as she is, she won't make it far anyway." *Allana must have broken free!* Re-invigorated, Evan twisted his body around so that he was dragged heels first. His captor took a step forward and Evan dug his heels in, dirt sinking beneath his feet. *Thump.* The grip on his wrist broke and Evan furiously crawled away trying to regain his feet as darkness enveloped him.

"Where'd he go? I should be able to see through this." Confused shouts bombarded Evan's ears and he glared at the ground. *Oh sure, now you start working.* He grumbled at his abilities. *Where is Allana?* He had regained his feet and broken into a run, he could see in the darkness he had produced, but that hardly helped him search for his friend. *I think I can take a little break now and figure out where I'm going.* He paused for a moment breathing deeply.

"Evan why are you stopping? They won't be distracted for long, move it!"

"Allana?" Evan whirled around, and there stood his bedraggled friend. He was skeptical, Shadow Court Fae had used this trick before.

"Yes, who do you think it is, now move it!" The look on her face and the tone was too familiar, *There's no way that's not her,* he realized, and rushed ahead, his friend limping after him.

Chapter Thirteen

Allana's heart was pounding so loud, she couldn't hear her feet striking the ground as she limped after Evan. With each step, she could feel an agonizing jolt shoot through her injured leg. *We need to find somewhere to hide, fast.* A glimpse of something shadowy caught her eye up ahead. The image of a Shadow Operative waiting to strike burst into her mind, and for a moment her heart seemed to lurch out of her chest. A moment later, she relaxed as she realized it was merely a caved- in spot at the base of a rocky outcrop. An idea leapt into her mind. "Evan!" she called, as quietly as she could.

The boy skidded to a halt and spun around with a frantic and questioning look on his face. "What is it?" Allana gestured frantically toward the cave. For a moment, Evan glanced blankly between her and the outcrop, looking confused. Then, squinting at the rocks, he seemed to realize. "Oh!"

Beckoning to him, Allana ducked into the tiny cave created by the outcrop. It was filled with unoccupied cobwebs and was slightly damp, but she hardly cared. A moment later, Evan ducked in beside her. Tucking herself as tightly as she could to the wall, Allana prayed the long grasses and ivy obscuring the entrance would keep them out of sight. Minutes passed, and Allana was beginning to wonder if they'd lost their pursuers when a deep, growly voice rang out nearby.

"Psh, managing to be outsmarted by some silly kids. Honestly, Arctos, I knew you weren't the sharpest dagger in the sheath but this is ridiculous —"

"Oh, shut up! I don't see you having any more success finding them."

Allana could hardly breathe as the voices of the Shadow Court Fae trailed closer and closer. *What if we left footprints? What if one of us dropped something? If they find us, there's no way we'll be able to escape after wedging ourselves in this hole.* Wild and frantic thoughts fluttered about in her head like caged birds, making her already spinning and aching head feel close to detonation. The deathly close crunch of gravelly dirt made even the fluttering thoughts in her head freeze. "Do you think they went this far in?" asked Arctos, his voice fading slightly as he turned back to address his comrade. "I mean, they're scared little kids. Wouldn't they have tried to double back and make a break for the border?"

"Maybe," growled the other Shadow Court Fae. "Either that, or they're hiding."

A chill ran down Allana's spine, an odd occurrence for a Winter Court Fae. *Don't look over here, don't look over here…*

"But if they were doing that, wouldn't they be farther back the way we came. The girl was injured, after all. I don't think she would've made it far in that state."

"Perhaps," muttered the other Fae. "Alright, we'll double back and check more thoroughly. We could really use Gaelin and his tracking abilities right now, the twerp got out of it somehow."

As their voices faded, Allana slowly let out the breath she'd been holding for the last minute. Slowly, the terror she'd felt began to ebb into feelings of stress and agitation. *What do we do now? My stupid leg is hurt, and those guys are crawling around like ants through here. Not to mention —* Rubbing her violently aching head, she shook herself restlessly out of her thoughts and glanced up at Evan. He was pinned up against the opposite wall, staring wide- eyed yet unseeing at the mouth of the hole they were hiding in. Evidently, he was still listening for them. "They're gone," said Allana, rather shortly. *Why can't he keep up?*

Evan turned to her, shaking and breathing heavily. He opened his mouth, as though to respond, but closed it again moments later. After several moments of silence, he seemed to perk up. "Wait, w—where's the other rucksack?" he croaked as he glanced around where he was sitting, his voice hoarse from breathing so hard.

Allana glanced around, her anger and fear rising as she saw it was missing. "Oh no, no, no, that had our food in it!" She slapped a hand to her forehead, stifling an angry groan as her head began to spin nauseatingly again. Through her fingers, she glared at Evan. "If we had any chance of making it, you just killed it!"

"Shhh! And if you talk any louder, we're as good as dead." Evan whispered frantically, slapping his hand over her mouth as he did so.

Allana was taken aback, but her anger was still hot so she pried his hand off her mouth and lowered her voice before continuing to berate him.

"And once they find it they'll be able to follow our footprints relatively well, which will ultimately lead them here."

"Maybe they won't find it." responded Evan, though he didn't sound like he believed it himself. "We could try going back after a while and looking—"

"Are you stupid?" snapped Allana, unable to hold in the frustration and stress that felt like it was boiling over inside of her. "Of course they'll have found it!" She wanted to pace, to punch something, to do anything but stay in the tiny, cramped hole and whisper-shout at the human who still somehow thought they had a chance. "Of all of the humans I had to be stuck with for this nonsense, it had to be the most average, unqualified creature of them all!"

Evan flinched sharply, as though she'd struck him. Surprise flashed through her, followed by a pang of regret; she hadn't really meant what she'd said. She opened her mouth, but Evan spoke first. "Quit using me as your punching bag!" he snapped back, his voice rising slightly. "This situation is just as much your fault as it is mine! You're acting as though everything wrong is my fault when you basically abandoned me in the middle of that fight!"

Allana's regret vanished into indignance. "I didn't abandon you! You were the one being an idiot and letting those guys beat you up even though you *literally* have the power of one of the greatest Fae in our land!" Frost crackled in her fists and dampened the ground around her.

"Again with the 'punching bag thing'!" responded Evan, his voice almost back to normal level. "We might've just blown the only chance Aeternum has, and all you're doing is just sitting here and telling me how stupid I am. If you're so smart, tell me, how are we gonna beat Verratyr if we can't even handle his soldiers? How?" Evan's voice, shaking with fear and anger, cut off. He lapsed into silence, breathing heavily and staring at Allana. His retort seemed more of a plea, a plea for an answer that Allana didn't have.

"I— I don't know," she said finally, her voice quiet. The painful silence stretched out like the lengthening shadows as the sun set. As darkness began to settle in, Allana became aware of the stinging pain in her leg. Glancing woozily down at it, she could see even in the half-light the blood seeping slightly through her pant leg. Sighing, she reached over and began to blindly fumble in the bag for the medical supplies she'd brought. *I'm glad we at least didn't lose these.* Tugging out some crumpled bandages, she began fumbling with them. Her head began to throb harder from even the small effort of sitting up, and nausea began to creep up her throat. Flopping back against the rock wall with an irritable huff, Allana rested her head against the cool stone and closed her heavy eyelids. *What if we did? What if we've actually let all of the Fae down? Have we already failed this quickly?* The remembranceof the confidence they'd had when talking to Athena the day before felt like a distant memory. *We were so naive to think we could actually do this.* As her headache began to subside, she became aware of something soft against her wounded leg. Blinking open her eyes, she could see in the gloom that Evan had taken the bandages and was trying his best to doctor up her injury. As she watched him quietly work, a twinge of sadness twisted her stomach. *After all of the nasty things I said to him, he's still willing to help me.* As she rested her head back against the rock, she couldn't shake the feeling that it was all her fault, not Evan's, that they'd failed.

* * * * *

Peering out into the darkness, Evan rubbed a hand through his hair wearily. *I don't think I've ever been more glad to be able to see in the dark. I wonder if that comes from the Shadow Heir power too —* He tried to concentrate as he listened out for approaching scouts, but his mind was far from focused on his task. Allana's words rang painfully in his ears. *'Of all of the humans I had to be stuck with for this nonsense, it had to be the most average, unqualified creature of them all.'*

He squeezed his eyes shut, trying to ignore the lump beginning to form in his throat. *I should have known from the beginning that I can't do anything worthwhile. Now, because I was stupid enough to think I could actually be something other than a boring, average person, hundreds of Fae have suffered, and my friend is hurt.* Blinking furiously as tears blurred the shafts of moonlight streaming into their hiding spot, he wiped his eyes with the back of one of his numb, scraped hands. *And to think, I thought I could've been like grandaddy one day —* He pulled his legs up closer to his body as a chilly breeze trickled in from the maw of the cave, resting his face against his knees. The tempting darkness of sleep began to envelop him.

"Can you tell me a story, granddaddy?"
Evan's eyes fluttered open to see a little boy peering cheerfully up at him. The child's eyes were a bright brown, and

strangely familiar. "Oh, of course, Evan!" He replied, his voice hoarse with age and filled with affection.

"Can you tell me one of those ones where you and your friends are fighting the bad guys?" Chirped the little child, settling himself on the couch next to Evan. "I like those ones."

Evan chuckled. "So do I. Let me think… Oh, I have one." He shifted himself with a grunt in his seat, settling against the plush backing of the couch. "So, our mission was to sneak around the enemy at night, when they couldn't see us. There were also lots of bushes and trees so, as long as we were quiet, we could have a chance. However, we had to stick together and work as a team in order to surround them without being spotted." He paused to grin at the young boy. The little one was looking up at him with an expression of rapt interest, his eyes wide with wonder and excitement. "We'd almost surrounded them when one of my comrades slipped while crossing a ditch and fell in. He didn't get hurt, but the noise was loud enough that a few guards came to investigate. Instead of panicking, my friend Jack and I began to hoist him out of the ditch. The enemy was quick, though. They were almost on top of us, and, if we didn't do something fast, we could blow the whole mission. So, instead of helping him climb out of the ditch, we carefully climbed in ourselves, and hid up against a bank under some big bushes. They came up to where we were hiding, and for a moment, I thought we were goners, but they passed over us. After they left, we all helped each other out and were able to surprise and defeat them. If we hadn't all stuck together and kept our heads, we would have failed."

"Wow!" cheered the little boy, bouncing in his seat. "I wanna be like you and your friends one day! Can you tell me another one? Pleeease?"

Evan laughed at his barrage of questions. "Sure!"

Oddly though, Evan's voice began to grow distant, and the scene began to fade from view. The warmth of the room and the nostalgic scent of firewood faded into that of chilly air and the sharp smell of pine needles —

His eyes fluttered open to the darkness of the chilly, dank cave. He sighed, rolling his shoulders, which were stiff from sitting against the rock. *Just a dream.* He glanced out through the ivy obscured entrance into the dark stretches of pine needles and grass beyond. *I guess that weird power memory thing applies to humans as well. I can remember grandaddy telling me that story.* As the memory of his grandfather telling him that story flooded back, nostalgia seemed to wash over Evan. He closed his eyes. For a moment, it seemed like nothing had changed; everything was fine, his grandad was alive, the world didn't seem to rest on his shoulders… He clung onto the feeling, mulling over the dream. As he sat curled against the wall in the silent darkness, a particular phrase seemed to resurface. *' If we hadn't all stuck together and kept our heads, we would have failed.'* Evan sat upright as realization seemed to hit him like a brick. *We only screwed up because we lost our heads and split up rather than sticking together. Maybe, if we do start working together, we might have a chance.* Hope seemed to flare within him once more. *Maybe we still can fix this.* He glanced over at Allana. The Fae was slumped back against the stone wall, her eyes closed and her face even paler than usual and tinged with green. A stab of worry shot through him. "Allana?"

"Mm?" The Fae blinked open one silvery white eye.

Evan paused, thinking about what to say. *I hope this makes sense.* "I had another one of those weird memory dreams again. One about my grandad."

"And?" mumbled the Fae, closing her eyes once more.

"Well, he used to be a soldier, and would tell me stories about how he and his comrades managed to survive some pretty crazy odds. They managed to survive situations that should have killed them by sticking together and working as one."

"Are you going somewhere with this?" muttered Allana groggily, rubbing the now black and blue bruise on her head.

"I'm getting there. We lost so badly to those guys because we both freaked out and abandoned each other the second they attacked. I think it would have gone differently if, instead of us each individually trying to 'save us' we had worked like a team, playing to each other's strengths and using the combined power to our advantage. What I'm trying to say is that if we're going to succeed, we're going to have to start working like a team and put our arguments about each other's shortcomings aside

"So you're saying we should try again based on the fact that a story your grandfather told you says you should?" Allana had opened her eyes and perked up slightly. Though her tone was incredulous, her eyes seemed contemplative.

"It's not just a silly story, it was something that really happened to him," Evan countered. "I would think you'd understand this just as much as I do. You've lived most of your life around the Fae Courts. Surely, they work better when they're working together rather than arguing over whether Summer Court should play drums or trumpets."

The corner of Allana's mouth twitched. She shifted her position slightly, looking pensive. "So, we give it another try, but work together cohesively, is that what you're saying?" She paused, then asked the question that seemed to be hanging in the air. "But what if it's still not enough?"

Evan faltered, the words sending a wave of doubt through his resolve. *What if it doesn't work? What will we do then? What will Fae do then?* Steeling himself, Evan met her gaze, forcing his voice to stay even. "It has to be. It's the only thing left we can do."

Allana turned her head slightly to peer outside; the sun was beginning to rise, and the inky blackness was slowly gaining a blue tint. After a moment, she sighed, and turned back to Evan. "Okay. We'll give it another shot, and work together this time." Then both of them lapsed into silence, the journey before them sitting heavily on their shoulders. The night was eerily quiet, the only sound was the occasional rustle of the evergreen trees in the wind and the gentle humming feeling that Evan had so often experienced while wandering Aeternum with Allana.

Finally, Allana spoke. "Look, I'm sorry for saying all of that nonsense to you. I guess you're kind of right about the punching bag thing. I didn't mean a word of it. I don't think any average human would take up the mantle of 'human that's being hunted down by shadowy acolytes and has strange unique shadow power' as well as you have, and I think you're way more capable than any other Fae give you credit for."

Evan was taken aback but flattered. "Oh, thank-" he faltered as Allana glanced up sharply. "er, sorry."

The frosty Fae snorted, unable to hide her amused grin.

"Alright, we'll need to move quickly. Since we have very little food, we can't really hesitate or fall back," Allana said, stuffing the medical supplies back into the bag. Some time had passed since their conversation, and a red and orange glow was now illuminating the sky and breathing life into the cold and eerie pine trees surrounding them.

"Okay," replied Evan. "How're you feeling?"

"Fine," said Allana, only half-truthfully. Her leg injury was throbbing painfully and felt very warm and, though her headache had subsided slightly, she feared what would happen if she tried to stand. "Alright, packed. Are you ready?"

"Ready as I'll never be," replied Evan, crawling from the hole. Allana followed suit, wincing as pain shot through her leg. The blinding sunlight in her eyes made her flinch once more as she clambered into the open. Straightening up, she felt the world lurch around her, and nausea leap into her throat.

Evan grasped her arm in a steadying hold. "Whoa, are you alright?"

Giving her woozy head a little shake, Allana turned to her friend. "Yeah, I'm fine, I probably shouldn't have gotten up so quickly." She adjusted the rucksack strap on her shoulder and glanced about. "Does the coast look clear?"

"We seem to be okay. I don't hear or see anything."

"I'll take it. Let's go."

After several minutes of slightly tense walking and checking behind trees and rocks, Allana was beginning to feel the strain of her injuries. Her headache was rapidly returning, and the vicious throbbing in her leg made it feel as though it were about to give out, feeling all the more prominent due to the dizziness accompanying the headache. She paused, leaning against a nearby pine with a sigh. *What I wouldn't do for some of that Uyu juice that Athena makes right now.*

"We're almost at the border!" called Evan over his shoulder. "I can feel it!"

We're so close, I can make it through this. Hoisting herself upright, Allana followed Evan's retreating form through the trees. The foliage and bushes began to grow thick and tugged painfully at Allana's skin and clothing. She was vividly reminded of when Elmer Gristle had chased her and Evan through the woods as they raced to get to Aeternum . *Gosh, that feels like eons ago. After all of the wildness we've been through, it feels like I've known Evan for a lot long —* "Oof!" Allana stumbled backward as she ran into Evan. "What did you stop for?"

"Look," muttered Evan, pointing upward. Allana glanced up and stifled a gasp. A massive, crumpling archway of very dark stone loomed before them, slightly obscured in ominous, twisted dead trees and attached on either side to equally deteriorated walls stretching as far as the eye could see. Inside the archway was a ring of mushrooms.

"This is it?" asked Allana, half-whispering as she gazed up at the foreboding archway.

"Yep." Evan took a deep breath. The two exchanged glances before wordlessly stepping into the unknown.

Chapter Fourteen

Evan strained his eyes, and blinked to adjust them. All manner of Cypress surrounded them, their needle like leaves blotting out all but the most determined sunbeams. His feet felt wet and he looked down to see that his sneakers were sunk in slightly marshy ground. Looking to his left, he saw Allana, hair plastered to her face and her clothes soaked through with water. *What the... how is she wet? I mean it's humid but it's not **that** humid.* Evan opened his mouth.

"Not a word, I'm not in the mood," Allana grumbled and tightened the knot of her red soaked bandage. Evan frowned, sweat was precipitating on her face, and pain shone in her eyes.

"I bet you could cool off if you gave yourself a snow flurry," he suggested.

"Why do you think I'm wet? I tried that as soon as we stepped through, it's so hot it melted, and so humid that it stayed." Allana began limping forward, her jaw was locked, and her breath came out in heavy gasps after a few steps. The red on her bandage deepened. *I can't let her keep on like that.* Walking down the narrow path, he caught up to her. He began to psyche himself up. *Just do it Evan, she needs you to stay alive so she can't murder you for this.* Taking a deep breath, he grabbed the arm swinging by her side and swung it over his shoulders, keeping a hand on her wrist while putting his other arm around her waist.

"Evan stop, I'm—" she yawned "fine." Allana shook her head in defiance. But Evan refused to back down. She tried to shove him off, he kept his grip firm, and her feeble attempt was thwarted. "Evan," she turned her head slowly and glared. *Sorry that won't work this time,* Evan thought and he glared right back, his mismatched eyes were glinting dangerously.

"I am not letting you limp around on a leg wound with a concussion. There's no way I can convince you to take a rest for a little bit so I'm helping you walk." Allana opened her mouth.

"Ah," he tutted. "We'll move faster, and you know it."

"Fine, but loosen your grip on my wrist. I don't need another injury to add to my list." His grip returned to a normal strength. Evan felt her lean on him and he could hear her feet begin to drag. Evan looked down at her, her eyes were blinking heavily and her head was nodding. *You're almost there, let yourself rest,* he thought worriedly. Sighing, he felt her dead weight fall onto him and a quick glance showed her eyes had slowly fallen shut.

Steadily they made ground. Silence reigned and the dark trees creaked in the warm breeze. Without the stimulus of conversation Evan was painfully aware of every discomfort, the beads of sweat slowly trickling down his face and back, the soggy soles of his shoes that were slowly soaking his socks and most of all the ever present gloom of his surroundings. Something about the tall trees that hung above them creeped Evan out. The leaves on the tree looked like wet seaweed and had bumps all over it. Evan shivered and kept on. There wasn't much of a path to follow so Evan wasn't really sure where he was going, he was leading on instinct alone. *Well, instinct's been the only way to do magic so far anyway.* He tried to assure himself but he was having trouble believing his own assurances. As time went on, Allana leaned more heavily on him and each of her steps became more and more lethargic, until Evan was almost dragging her. *We'll have to stop soon. I can't keep carrying her like this.* With this thought he began to look for a suitable campsite.

He sighed with relief. In front of him was an enormous cypress tree with a wide hollow opening in the trunk, large enough for both himself and his companion to lodge in. His shadow vision allowed him to check for animals, though he didn't know why he bothered. *It's not like we've seen or heard any animals since we got here, or that any would want to live in such a dark climate.* Grunting, he laid the sleeping Allana on the ground. He stretched his aching shoulder muscles, then pushed Allana into a sitting position, squatting he wrapped his arms around her torso and grabbed his own wrist. Leaning back he stood and began to drag her into the tree.

Sleep was elusive, the inside of the tree was more comfortable than he expected but that still set it pretty low on the comfort scale. Allana, due to her concussion had been out for hours, he found himself wishing he had a concussion if only to get a solid night's rest. He shifted on the ground, how long it took for his eyes to finally slide shut he didn't know. But not even his exhausted body could subdue the horror in his mind.

No.. no… no… tears streamed down his face. Slowly, he managed to crawl over to Jack's body. He laid his head on his friend's chest and wept, whispering "Why wasn't it me? Why wasn't it me?" With this last word his world went black. His spirit seemed to leave his body and he was watching himself, or rather, his grandfather. How did Granddaddy survive? A bomb landed right on top of them, yet he only came out with a mild bout of chest pain… He groaned. You know what, dream? I'm too tired to care. My Grandaddy survived and got to meet me and teach me all sorts of cool but practical things, like some of his survival skills. It doesn't matter how he got out of that situation and I am way too tired to care, so shut up and let me sleep. That seemed to quiet his mind and slowly he drifted off to more pleasant dreams.

Evan woke with the vague sense that he was in danger. *I'm probably just jumpy from my nightmare.* He tried to fall back asleep, but he couldn't shake the feeling. His sore muscles groaned in protest as he quickly heaved himself off the ground. Stepping through the hole in the trunk, Evan couldn't tell whether it was day or night, a problem that had occurred to him the day before.

"Finally, I thought you'd never wake up." Evan whirled around, his heart nearly leaping straight out of his chest. In front of him was a black haired, green eyed Fae that was taller than Evan by a good foot, with a mischievous glint in his eyes. His attire was made up of black pants, a dark gray undershirt with a black leather jerkin and a sword hung from a leather sheath.

"Get back," Evan warned, trying to summon some form of power.

"Relax, I'm not here to hurt you."

"And I'm supposed to believe you because?" Evan narrowed his eyes.

"Because I know where Veratyrr is, and I can get you to him quickly." A certain smugness entered his voice, that set off Evan's mental warning signals.

"My friend and I are getting on just fine."

"Which is why she's currently passed out inside a tree trunk with an infected injury and a severe concussion." Evan opened his mouth, but the Fae cut him off. "Yes I've been tailing you, it wasn't hard. You have a very unique magical signature. Evan snapped his mouth shut. *There's no way he's telling the truth, but if he really does lead us there we don't have a choice. We have to get to Veratyrr and end this.*

"And if I say no to your offer?"

"You'll die without me helping you along anyway."

"I'll have to discuss it with my friend."

"I'll be waiting."

Evan slowly backed into the tree trunk never taking his eyes off the Fae in front of him.

"Allana, there's a—" *Where is she?* Out of his peripheral vision, he had seen where Allana had been, but her body no longer sat there. He jerked his eyes away from the Shadow Fae and searched around the tree. She was gone. *No no no.*

* * * * *

Veratyrr chuckled. When he had murdered the May Queen, he had expected the full wrath of the Courts to reign down on him, especially after that imbecile Gristle revealed his plans to his welp of an enemy. Instead, two children were wandering through his lands, his adversary practically dragging an injured girl, who must have been his friend, through the woods. He grumbled impatiently. No anxiety plagued him, for he knew his confrontation with the children would be short and easy, but he wanted it over so he could move on to bigger things with the power he was due. *Once this is over, I can focus on making sure a May Queen does not arise. After this, I will be without question the most powerful Fae in existence.* He laughed, an eerie, cruel sound that echoed against the stone walls around him. The girl was unconscious and now the boy really was forced to drag his friend. His shade wolf was trailing them closely, and whatever he saw, Verratyr saw. *Oh the plans I have for you.*

Chapter Fifteen

Allana opened her eyes, stone walls encapsulated her, *great I've moved again. And Evan is nowhere to be found.* On further examination, she saw that she was in a prison, bars formed a door on her right side. *Not good.* She slid towards the bars, her leg aching too much to attempt to stand, and reached the lock. She racked her brain for a way to escape, but no ideas came to her. *I must be in Veratyrr's palace, but why me? Not Evan, unless he's dead… No, there's no way he can be. He has enough instinct to keep him alive, and if Evan was dead there would be no reason to keep me here as possible leverage. If I could just escape, I could end it right here…* Allana flicked snowflakes into the air. She was so used to the dull ache of her leg that her concentration was no longer hindered by it and was able to keep them frozen. One by one the snowflakes fell and right before the last one hit the cool stone floor, she sent up another spark of flakes. She absently repeated this for what must have been hours until one landed on the lock.

Frozen? Of course! Duh. I should have thought of that earlier. Struggling to her knees, she stuck her hand to the keyhole and sent a blast of ice on and in the lock. She kept up a steady stream until she felt the metal beneath would be cool enough. Then, with extreme difficulty, she made a hammer out of ice. Listening to make sure no one was walking down the hallway, she took the hammer in both hands and whacked it against the brittle lock. The hammer shattered as did the ice on the lock, but when tested, the door was still well fastened. Sighing, she repeated the process. Her gray hands were clammy. She groaned as she formed yet another brittle ice hammer. *Bang, crack!* Her hammer broke, the lock stayed unmoved. Her fingers were lanced with pain, taking a deep breath, she attempted to extend them.

"Agch!" She clutched her hands to her chest. Hours of sitting in an unreasonably hot and humid cell had made her hands swollen and beefy, the swelling cramping her hands into permanent hammerfists. Hyperthermia was slowly taking over her body and the simple act of extending her fingers was too much for her exhausted and overheated body. Desperately she tried to make another icey tool, but her hands were so tightly swollen that all her attempts to make a hammer in them had failed. Allana grit her teeth. *Come on Allana, you can do this, one more time. Just move your fingers.* Concentrating, she fought to move them. A sharp cramping pain shot up her arms and into her neck. She sucked in a breath as her eyes watered furiously, warm salty tears slowly sliding down her lowered face. Allana was oblivious to all passage of time, but however much passed it was enough to dry her tears and fuel her anger. Standing, she glared at the door, ice still coated the lock. *Stupid lock, why won't you just break?* All of the impatience and anger at her own pain seemed to explode from her as she jumped and snap kicked the lock. "Ow!" She clutched her thigh hopping on one foot as horrific, white- hot pain scorched through it. *Of course I forgot and kicked with my injured leg- creak.-* Allana turned her head towards the door. Slowly the door continued to groan until it at last swung open.

* * * * *

He ran outside "You. Where is she." Evan clipped off every word and leaned into the Fae's personal space.

The Fae stood up. "My name is Gaelin, do you mean to say she's gone?"

"Don't play that game with me. Where is she?" The Fae walked away and into the tree. He looked closely at the ground and enveloped it with shadows. When they dissipated, paw prints were visible on the ground.

"It's Veratyrr. He sent his Shade wolf and took her."

"Shade wolf?" Evan was skeptical.

"It's an animal, found in the shadow lands. Only very powerful Fae can tame them, and use their power."

"And I'm supposed to trust that you didn't just set this all up?"

"If I was going to capture one of you, I would have done it while you were both asleep. If your friend is going to live through the night you need to follow me."

"Why would you help me? If you can read my magic signature or whatever you must know that I have your leader's power," Evan asked, slightly proud of himself for somewhat understanding the magic knowhow his acquaintance had spouted.

"That is a very complicated question, with a long winded answer, in simple terms my leader is not exactly, how shall I put it? beloved by his subjects or his inner circle, due to his *style* of ruling. Your friend's life is wasting as we speak," he prodded.

Evan thought for a moment then nodded. "Fine, but I want you walking ahead of me." Evan insisted.

"If you insist" he sneered and started walking. "Come along, human."

Even if he isn't lying if he says 'human' like that again I'm going to show him exactly how we humans forced the likes of him into hiding.

Despite Evan's mental threat, he did not end up strangling his temporary ally, though, he had to suffer through many more 'come along humans' before the benefits of his diplomacy came to fruition. Evan's feet were aching by the time they reached their destination, and his shoulder still ached from having to carry Allana's deadweight the day before. They seemed to be taking no particular path, and it was many hours before they at last reached a ring of black and green mushrooms with silvery light streaming into the center.

"Here we are. The entrance to the palace grounds," Gaelin said, and pulled Evan into the marshy middle of the ring. Cold and warmth seemed to be warring in Evan's body for control. Sunlight and moonlight poured through his veins, and the more they fought the faster his body was hurled to a blinding light. He squinted and braced for impact, but remembered Allana's words. *If you refrained from tensing you would be able to stick the landing.* With great effort he relaxed. And to his delight when he opened his eyes, his feet were placed firmly on the ground. *Finally! I was really getting tired of landing on my face.* After congratulating himself he took a scan of his surroundings. Weeping cypress made a wall around huge black gates. Behind that was a dreary, black, stone castle. The dark was suffocating but Evan's eyes seemed to adjust automatically now, using his Fae given ability when necessary. Shadow guards lined the entrance, swords, maces, and all other manner of weapons were shown on the well armed guards. Gaelin turned around and made a shushing motion with his fingers before enveloping Evan in shadows with the flick of one ash-colored hand. He then grabbed Evan's wrist and walked towards the front gate.

"Who is it?" A voice called.

"Gaelin."

"What do you have with you?"

"The usual."

"Carry on." The sound of creaking gates told Evan that they were opening and he couldn't believe how easy it had been. *Unless this is all a giant set up to get me killed. No, I can't think that, it's too late to second guess myself now. Besides, I would have had to figure out a way to get in here anyway.* A painfully long amount of time dragged by before Evan was removed from the cloud of darkness. When Gaelin removed it, they were standing behind the North wing of the castle. By the smell the stables seemed to be located on that side.

"Your friend will most likely be in the dungeon, the plan is to sneak down there and-"

"Hold on a minute, for all I know you could be sending me down there to put me in jail yourself, how do I know that you're not ly—" Gaelin spoke up harshly.

"Take one look around this place human, you think my goal is to trap you in a dungeon? My country is becoming destitute, you have the power to-"

"Ahhh!" A woman's scream of pain split through the air.

Evan's heart seemed to freeze in his chest as the rest of his sentence died in his throat. He knew that voice. "Allana." Evan croaked in breathless terror, racing towards the sound, which appeared to be coming from the other side of the castle. He didn't wait for Gaelin, for all Evan knew waiting could mean the difference between life and death. He rounded the corner and gasped. The unmistakable form of Allana was pinned to the wall by a horribly tall figure in large, menacing black wings, blood streaming down her arms, a sword pressed to her throat.

* * * * *

Veratyrr grinned menacingly at her, and slowly brought the sword to her throat.

"I remember you. The young maid who was talking to the Queen before I killed her. From what I heard, you two seemed close, no? Perhaps it will comfort you to know that you will soon be delivered to her arms again by the same hand and sword that took her out of yours."

Allana steeled her heart, and faced the sword with all the calmness she could possibly muster. No matter her fate, the murderous coward before her would not be given the satisfaction of seeing her fear. *He has already seen pain, but fear I will not allow. I have to get out of his grip.* She tried to think of ways to escape, but her injured leg was all but useless to either attack her foe or brace herself with. Her arms were covered in small knife slashes her assailant had wielded previously before drawing his other weapon to the point that attacking with them would not only cause serious pain, but enough blood loss that the effort would be pointless. Veratyrr looked to his right and smirked.

"Ahh, look who's here. You have ten seconds to give me what I want before she dies. But who can say what harm I'll do to her while I wait." Malicious intent oozed from his voice as he pulled out a dagger and put the cold blade against her pale gray cheek. Allana turned her head in the same direction as her captor. Mismatching eyes met hers from several yards away.

"Evan don—"

"Silence, welp!"A shadowy gag appeared over her mouth stopping the noise of her voice quite thoroughly. *Don't do it, don't do it don't do it…*

Chapter Sixteen

Evan stood, tensed, unable to move, his heart pounding so violently in his chest that he thought it might burst. The murderous Fae glared at Evan through the darkness cast by the cloud covered sky, and the natural shadow that seemed to coat all of the Shadow Cout terrain. Fighting the rising panic within him, Evan internally cursed himself. *Of course the other Shadow Court Fae can see in the dark like I can. Why didn't I think of that?* Despite his instinct to keep his eyes locked on his adversary, Evan chanced a glance at his surroundings. They seemed to be in some sort of courtyard. A grimy, metal-barred gate lined every edge of the dim unkempt courtyard. Several scruffy crows peered down at Evan from the walls, seeming almost entertained by the tense exchange. In the shadows of the woods, Evan spotted movement that made his heart frantically lurch.

Something dark was slowly circling them both. For a moment, the pitch black, wraithlike form of a colossal, shaggy wolf slunk from the shadows, a snarl pulling back its unnaturally black jowls. Despite its obvious wolf-like appearance, there was something ghostly and unclear about its outline, as though it were made up of the darkness cast throughout the area. *Considering some of the stuff I've seen while in Aeternum a wolf made of shadows doesn't seem out of the question at all.* Evan watched in horror as the beast's smoky, hazy outline prowled mesmerizingly forward, passing behind Veratyrr and Allana with its luminous white gaze fixed on its human quarry. There was a pleased gleam in Verratyr's eyes as he watched Evan squirm at the sight of his companion. With a light flick of one of his ashen, bony hands, the wolf's glowing pupil-less eyes vanished, and the creature swirled into nothing more than dark vapor that sank away into the surrounding gloom of the woods

Evan, realizing his mouth had been hanging slightly open in silent horror for the tense few seconds, shut it and fought to steady his fast, shallow breathing. Forcing himself to meet Verratyr's gaze, he tried to ignore the dank, clammy feeling of the atmosphere that did nothing to soothe his nerves and caused goosebumps to bloom across his arms. For a brief moment, he resisted the urge to glance over his shoulder, wondering if Gaelin might come assist him, but the idea seemed ludicrous. *He might have been a huge help with getting me in, but facing the ruthless king of the Shadow Court for a random human he just met is a ton more risky than just covering me in some Shadow magic and smuggling me past a few bored guards.*

"Are you going to dawdle forever, human? Because I don't think your friend has forever for you to think about whether to save your skin or not," smirked Veratyrr in a deadly growl that sent chills down Evan's spine. His heart jolted as he saw Verratyr press the dagger closer to Allana's throat, his eyes flashing menacingly. The Winter Court Fae froze in her efforts to wriggle free, her ghostly, hatred-filled eyes fixed on Veratyrr's face.

Taking a deep breath, Evan felt the power in his fingertips beginning to tingle in anticipation. *Shadow power, don't fail me now.* He could feel his hands violently shaking, but his mind was strangely calm. Slowly, he stepped from the shadows. Despite the humidity in the air, his throat was oddly dry as he spoke. "What do you want from me?"

"Ah, finally," sneered Veratyrr, drawing himself up to a frightening height and glancing over Evan through sickly green eyes in the sort of way a bird of prey might size up its quarry. To Evan, he was reminiscent of a nightmare incarnate; his smoke-colored form wreathed in a dark cloak seemed to vanish into the cold shadows of the dark stone, and his eyes glinted from the blackness like tiny knives. The huge ebony wings that loomed on either side of the Shadow Fae's frame seemed slightly tattered, as though the many unnecessary battles they'd doubtless been put through had done a number on them. Though they looked in shape and pattern like the cheerful monarch butterflies that often fluttered outside Evan's home, their dark, grayscale tone and shredded appearance made them seem corrupted and formidable. The fear that Gristle had instilled in him suddenly seemed like child's play. "Aeternum's most *heroic* last hope. Have you come to kill me, put me in my place?" He swung the short sword slightly as he spoke, and Evan fought the urge to wince at the sharp, blood-chilling *whoosh* it made as it cut through the air. "Adorable. Now, give me the power or she's dead."

The Shadow Court Fae gently rested the tip of the blade on Allana's face, watching with despicable relish as the wounded Winter Court Fae winced at its touch. The jet black metal of the sword seemed unnaturally dark, and though he had no idea why, Evan had the peculiar and horrible feeling that for it to cut her skin in any way would be a death sentence. *I have to stall until I can think of a plan.* Evan drew himself up taller, trying desperately to look confident. "You're acting awfully self-assured for someone who's weaker than me. I have your father's power; that makes me the most powerful one here," he said. *Yikes, I hope I sounded a lot braver than I think I sounded.*

Verratyr's eyes flashed, and he bared his teeth. Though still gripping Allana tightly with his hand and the menacing wisps of shadows that prevented her from speaking, he turned slightly to face Evan with ill-concealed rage. "Are you threatening me, human, with the fact that my father made the pathetic decision to give *my* rightful power to you? With the fact that you possess a power that you know nothing about nor how to use?'

"Heck yeah," Evan snapped back. His voice was slightly higher than normal. *Don't let him see how scared you are.*

"And clearly, I know how to use it. Haven't I escaped your men like four, five times now?"

"Oh, so sheer luck counts as using the power, does it?" The Shadow heir looked absolutely livid as he curled his lip. "I speak of truly using it, human, of *deserving* it. I've fought for that power, done everything that I can to learn about it, strived to wield it since the very moment it was spoken of to me. I am more deserving of that power than you could ever dream of being!"

"Who says that fighting for it means you're deserving of it?" countered Evan, searching desperately for things to stall with while he concocted a plan. "This power is supposed to be given to the Shadow Court leader, right? Last time I checked, real leaders don't run around murdering possible allies and oppressing their people." For a moment, the gruesome memories of the torched castle and the look on Thea's face as her life was snuffed out drifted into mind, and he felt anger pulse through his veins. The memories brought with them a wave of boldness. *I can't let that happen to anyone else I care about. We need to get rid of him.* He took a cautious step forward.

Verratyr snorted coldly. "Honestly, I knew humans were pitifully stupid, but even you've surpassed my expectations on how wretched they can be. I've killed the May Queen and brought my people to the top, above all of the other weaklings who are reliant on the silly ideals that you call 'real leadership'."

"You haven't brought your people to the top; you've only brought yourself." Evan thought of Gaelin, and how risky it had been to even help him get this far. *Things must be pretty rough for the Shadow Court citizens if he's willing to risk going against Veratyrr just for a chance that I might be able to stop him.* "I've seen what you've done to them. How do you think I managed to get in? Your own people respect you so little because of what you've done that they're willing to risk their skins to help me get rid of you."

For a moment, the Fae seemed slightly shocked, as though the notion of some of his people working against him was something he hadn't considered. However, the expression quickly faded into indifference. "Don't talk about things you don't understand, you weak- hearted creature. I don't need the respect of a bunch of cowardly fools to rule them, I only need the power to rule over them. Speaking of which." Verratyr turned back to Allana, holding the dagger so that it was dangerously close to her throat and meeting Evan's gaze with a cruel excitement in his eyes, his anticipation to receive the power that he so clearly wanted more than anything nearly tangible. "Give it to me, *now.*"

As Verratyr turned back to his quarry, Evan's mind raced with his next course of action. *What do I do? Even if I did know how to give him the Shadow heir power, I know he'll just kill me and Allana both once I give it to him, and then Aeternum will be doomed. Argh, but I can't just let Allana die! She's my friend, and she has to live, I know she has to…* He frantically recalled the dream he'd had of Verratyr and Tablarye. *Tablarye managed to escape him using this same power, but how did he do it? Everything I've done with it has kind of been an accident!* He knew that Verratyr was right, he knew hardly anything about his abilities, but Allana's life was in the balance, failure was a risk he was going to have to take. Fighting the urge to pace, he glanced up at Allana.

The Fae's glassy silver eyes, peering over the shadowy gag covering her mouth, seemed to silently beg him to flee, to save himself. Verratyr's words rang in his mind. *'Who can say what I'll do to you while I wait.' If I don't do something quickly, who knows what he'll do to her while I make my decision.* His gut lurched awfully as the gruesome decision tore at him. As Evan watched a bead of blood trickle down the side of her face, the memory of his other dream rushed back into his mind. The image of Jack's mangled body and the sound of his own sobs repeated painfully within his brain as the horrific recollection of his grandfather's memory flooded vividly back into mind.

He recalled his and Jack's cheerful banter moments before the tragedy had struck, and the rush of adrenaline that had accompanied the blast that followed. As the scarring memory washed over him once more, he was struck by the memory of the strange, electric jolt he'd felt when he had been sent flying. It felt strangely familiar, as though he himself had experienced it. *For some reason, it kind of reminds me of when Gristle — Oh!* Evan nearly gasped aloud as the truth struck him. The sensation he'd felt when he'd dreamt of Jack's death, the surging gush of power that had jolted up his arms to shield his body from harm. *That's how he lived; granddaddy used his power to survive the blast.* His heart began to pound so hard that he was sure that everyone in the courtyard must be able to hear it. Glancing at the evilly glinting blade in Verratyr's hand, Evan felt hope flare in him once more, burning away at the fear and the worry that was clouding his mind. *If Grandaddy could survive that explosion because of this power, I can survive a little sword. After all, I've had time to learn a little about how to use it.* Memories of using his power flooded into his mind, and a plan took form. Squeezing his hands into fists, Evan tensed. *I can save her, I know I can.*

"*Now, human!*" snarled Verratyr, a deadly hiss in his voice. He squeezed Allana's throat tighter, and the Fae writhed hopelessly against his grip. "Give it to me now, or I'll kill her and take it from you!" The Fae drew back the weapon to end Allana's life. And Evan lunged with all of the courage he could muster.

Slamming into the Fae, Evan instantly felt his breath driven out of him. Gulping for air, he caught a glimpse of flashing metal and grasped for the hand holding the short sword, gripping Verratyr's wrist as tightly as he could. He willed the power to come to him. It flooded into his fingers, spurring his hope onward. Suddenly, the hand on Verratyr's wrist was ripped free, and he found himself face to face with the Fae. His unnerving eyes were filled with a wild, vicious energy as he drew back his weapon. Evan saw the blade glint murderously in the light of the sun and felt the power expand out of his body creating a halo around him. The shadowy aura surged toward Verratyr, who lifted a hand. With a sharp stroke, shadows flew from his own fingertips, tackling the black mass and flinging it into nothingness. Evan only had a fraction of a second to watch his last hope whisp into nothing before he felt a claw like hand lock unto his shoulder and a hard jolt in his torso. Gasping and stumbling slightly, he tried to shove Veratyrr away, fighting to throw off the odd feeling that something was horribly wrong. Oddly, the Fae didn't seem to be on the offensive anymore. Though still gripping Evan by the arm, he was staring at him through eyes lit up with triumph, and a cruel grin was beginning to twist the corners of his mouth. Suddenly, Evan became aware of a fiery heat beginning to creep through his chest, as though someone had lit a match right next to his heart. His mind utterly blank, he followed the path of Verratyr's outstretched arm, his eyes coming to rest on an ebony hilt, the only visible remnant of the inky black short sword plunged deep into his chest.

An eternity felt like it had passed. He couldn't pull his eyes away from the blade, he couldn't take in what he was seeing. Despite how frantically his mind had been working mere seconds ago, it was now devoid of anything but the image before him. With a sharp jerk, Verratyr yanked the sword free. The motion sent another burning jolt through Evan's body. Stumbling forward and fighting for breath, Evan placed a hand over the wound, which came up a nauseating dark red. As he watched the blood bloom outward across his shirt alarmingly quickly, a wave of weakness seemed to drag him downward. He was only dimly aware of the sharp pangs in his knees as they hit the stone ground, all he could seem to focus on were the deep crimson droplets pattering unto the stone. An odd sucking feeling was beginning to pull at the corners of his consciousness, as though something were slowly pulling his life away from him. It reminded him of the strange, buzzing feeling he'd occasionally felt wandering through the rest of Aeternum, only it felt vicious and unfriendly, like someone was pulling him somewhere against his will.

Fighting to keep from collapsing completely to the ground, Evan tried to take in the truth of what had just happened. *It didn't work. I failed.* His thoughts felt numb and empty as he watched his own blood leak across the cold stone floor. *I'll never be able to see my family ever again.* He tried to push himself back up, hopelessly fighting the reality that he couldn't accept. I'll never *be able to go home.* He tried to gasp for air, but every breath felt like it was being pulled back away from him by the same horrible sucking feeling robbing his life. *I'll never be able to graduate, I'll never see Noel grow up. It's all over.* His thoughts trailed off as a strange feeling seemed to sweep over him. A sensation he knew well, a soft sunny feeling, was growing stronger and stronger. It was the all too familiar sensation he'd been feeling on and off since he'd entered Aeternum, the peculiar humming he'd felt when around… Peering through unfocused eyes, Evan saw Allana slumped against the wall several feet away. Verratyr had released his hold on her, and she stared at Evan, eyes wide, mouth stretched open in the remains of a horrified silent scream. No longer was the Fae trying to conceal her emotions, trying to seem like she didn't care; Evan could see even through his blurring vision the fear and grief flooding into her eyes. In that moment he saw how she truly truly saw him, he was her friend, best friend even. *She's my friend too, I-I really wanted to see the rest of this place with her.* The humming had grown into almost a song, and, despite the grueling heat and pain coursing through Evan's body, he could feel a peculiar, comforting warmth, as though a shaft of sunlight had struck the back of his neck. *It's like a – Oh!* The realization struck Evan harder than the knife. Suddenly, everything made sense. *All this time, I knew that feeling had to mean something. I just didn't realize – she's the –* His thoughts were cut short as the violently shaking arm supporting his body collapsed. With an agonizing jolt, he hit the stone floor. Darkness crept into the edges of his vision, and the horrible sucking feeling grasped at him. Fighting for breath, Evan squeezed his eyes shut against the pain.

"N-no." A nearby voice drew Evan's attention. Forcing one eye open, he could see Allana's pale grey face peering down at him, her eyes glistening. "Come on," she croaked in a whisper of failing determination.. "You've got to get up, we—" Her voice trailed off as her shoulders began to shake, tears leaking from her eyes. "I should never have agreed for us to come here, this is my fault. Please, don't go. I can't lose you too."

Evan felt his heart twist painfully, and opened his mouth to speak, though the only sound that came out was a hacking cough from the blood clogging his throat. . He gazed at his friend, fighting the tempting drowsiness that was coaxing him ever closer. *Poor Allana, I wish there was something I could say to help her.* Despite the dull agony of knowing he was dying twisting his insides, the comfort of knowing the truth brought an odd peace to him. He fought back another cough."Hey, it's okay. This isn't your fault. It was my idea." Drawing in a rattling breath, Evan tried to keep his eyes open as bitter tears stung them. *There's so much I want to thank her for. I wish I could tell her everything.* Fighting for enough air to speak, he met Allana's pale, tear-filled gaze. "I guess I've repaid you now. So I can say it. Thank you Allana, for everything," he managed a watery smile, before taking a shuddering breath.

Tears dripped down the Fae's face as she hung her head, shaking. Evan's heart twisted even tighter. He tried to lift a hand to offer her some sort of comfort, but his arm didn't have the strength. The malignant, sucking feeling was tugging harder and harder at him, blacking out the corners of his vision and making everything feel far away. "It'll be okay," he said, his voice now a mere raspy whisper. "It really will. I promise." Peering over Allana's shoulder, he saw Verratyr watching from several feet away with a look of mocking triumph on his face.

You have no idea what's coming. In spite of himself, Evan smiled, intently holding the Fae's gaze. For a moment, he thought he saw Verratyr's sneer falter. The sucking feeling was overpowering now, seeming to tug at his whole body. Fighting to see through the darkness swamping his vision, Evan met Allana's silvery eyes. The agony of leaving was worse than the pain from his wound. Summoning up the last of the air in his feebly working lungs, he earnestly gazed at the Fae who'd kept him alive and been his friend through so much, desperately hoping that somehow she'd see it in his eyes that all was not lost. "You'll be ok, everyone will. Trust me," he pleaded. He thought he saw Allana open her mouth to respond, but the darkness was finally blotting out the world around him. It swirled closer and closer, and the world vanished into blackness.

Chapter Seventeen

Something about that smile made Verratyr's skin crawl. *Why is he so smug? I've won, the Winter Court welp certainly can't stop me. So why did he smile?* It nagged at him, but he pushed the worry away. He felt power grasp his hands as it buzzed from his head all the way to his feet. He felt strange and peculiar, but it was an excellent feeling, it pulsed within his veins, eager to be used by its *rightful* owner. He began to smirk, and the image of Evan smiling came to mind, and worry wormed itself into his triumph. No, no way he was going to let something so small bother him, after everything he had gone through, no. *I'm acting ridiculous, I won't let that child's face mar my victory.* He looked over to the Fae girl and the boy. She was weeping, almost out of breath. The human, eyes closed, turned to the sky. He didn't feel any regret for doing this. He felt nothing except power. Or at least, that's what he thought this feeling might be. Even so, he still found himself thinking about the smile the boy had given the Winter Court Fae before fading away.

How and why would anyone smile at that moment? Was he just seeing things? Maybe it was a mistake. He felt like maybe the boy felt content even after feeling that pain. He was still content. How could someone like him possibly be content with a horrible fate like the one he had just experienced? Veratyrr had never been content, contentment led to weakness and stagnation. In the Shadow Court weakness was not tolerated. *Nor should it be.* But curiosity plagued him. How could the human have been content knowing that his efforts had been useless and that his friend was soon to die in the same manner he had? Verratyr wanted to know how this was possible. But he didn't have time to think about it. The young girl was charging him, rage in her eyes. He felt a grin spread across his face. *I'll let her suffer a bit longer.* It's not like she could fight anyway. She was only weak, nothing else. She was no threat to him.

   She threw large, sharp icicles at him, yawning, he threw up a shadow barrier. The ice shattered against it. As he lowered the barrier, the foolish girl leaped at him, a dagger in hand. Reaching into the air he grabbed her ankle and slammed her into the ground. A groan rose from the dust beneath him and he smirked again. *I'm rather enjoying myself. I think I'll let her try at it for a bit longer.* The girl rose to her feet, panting, she charged again. This time Veratyrr didn't let her get close; he blasted her with shadow and sent her sailing into the ground next to her friend's body.

* * * * *

   Allana's body ached. She should've been more cautious. She had wanted revenge so badly she hadn't even thought before she charged. But her enemy had given her painful reminders to think before she leaped. Looking up she saw that she had landed next to Evan. She felt helpless, trapped for a moment without anyone to turn to but her lonely thoughts. *Why did I bring you here? If I had just taken you straight back to where you came from none of this would have happened, you'd still be here.* Though she desperately wanted to look away, she couldn't tear her eyes from the limp form of her friend lying still next to her. Hot tears kept streaming down her cheeks, never stopping. She felt like she couldn't possibly let Evan go but she knew she had to, just for a little bit. She glared up at the despicable evil hovering a few feet away, leering delightedly at her pain. She thought maybe Veratyrr felt content after getting what he wanted. She could barely even look him in the eyes without wanting to fight him. That's exactly what she was going to do. But this time more wisely. She could sense something inside her that she'd never

183

felt. As she put Evan's body down, she stood up, very slowly, and stood there. A memory came to the front of her mind. A moment when the May Queen told her she would be something worthwhile.

Was this what she meant? Did she know this would happen this whole time? That was impossible, right? Nothing made sense to Allana anymore. She couldn't handle all of this at once, everything rushing to her so fast. She felt like the world around her was moving as she stood. She was shaking all over. She couldn't help but let her tears fall. *You got what you wanted, didn't you? You monster, leave us alone. You've done enough. More than enough.* She found herself repeating those words in her mind. Evan hadn't deserved this. She just wished he would come back. It was too early for him to leave so soon. *You took him away from me. You took everyone away from me. Rosela, Thea, and now Evan. And if you win you're going to take so many more from so many Fae.* She breathed hard and long and rage filled her. Power flared all across her. *This needs to be stopped now before anyone else gets hurt. You already took enough away from me, and the rest of the world.*

She didn't mean for any of this to happen. She felt fire fill her head. She felt as if she could faint right now on the floor. So much anger made her sick to her stomach. She wanted to feel comfort and nothing else. She knew that if she let him win, all of Aeternum would fall under his rule. The May Queen had told her she would do something worthwhile. *It's now or never.* Allana looked over at him preparing to fight. Why was he looking all over the place? He couldn't back out now. Not after all he did. He couldn't escape. She wouldn't allow it. She didn't even know where this feeling came from but she never felt more powerful in her life. At the same time, she felt weak. Walking into this battle without her cheerful friend at her side, filling her with hope via his endless enthusiasm and determination. She took a step toward him. He flinched. No, he couldn't be scared of her all of a sudden. *What happened? He was so powerful but suddenly he doesn't want*

to fight anymore? This makes no sense. I don't understand him.
Why is he scared?

Pain flared through her back and a buzzing filled her
ears. Her back felt heavier, she turned her head back, and
gasped. Giant multi-colored morpho menelaus Butterfly
wings stretched behind her. *The buzz, the power rush, his
smile… I'- I- I'm the next May Queen. Oh Evan, why couldn't you
have just realized sooner… It's all my fault you're gone.* She took a
deep breath, *He died because he knew you could do this, and he was
right.*

She took a step forward, getting into a fighting
position. Nothing could stop her now. *Evan, I know you're
listening. Thank you for everything. I'm going to fight for you. One
day we will see each other again, but for now I need to win this
battle. Evan, this is for you.*

Verratyr watched as Allana struggled to get up. His
grin faded as he felt a strange feeling come across him. *What is
this?* With a flash of brilliant blue and indigo, shimmering
wings burst from the girl's shoulders, unfurling to their full
size. A roaring hum buzzed through Verratyr's body, shaking
away his confusion as reality hit him. *No.* He felt a wave of
dread wash over him, flinging away his certainty and triumph
and coiling furiously around his insides. *No, not her, that
insignificant child? It can't be. All of my hard work, all of the risks I
took, for this to happen?* Suddenly, the boy's dying smile and his
odd words of comfort made sense as the realization of what
he'd just unleashed poured over him like molten rock. *Does
she realize? She has giant wings blossoming from her back, of course
she realizes.* His thoughts went all over the place. No, he
couldn't fight. Was there an escape maybe? He looked around
him, looking for something to help, maybe to distract her
with. He never, until this very moment, knew that the young
Fae who'd been traipsing about alongside his quarry would
be his greatest threat, and she was the next May Queen,
hiding in plain sight. He felt weak. He thought Allana was the
weak one but after this he felt the tables had turned, she

would defeat him. He couldn't have this. He had to win. He couldn't back out any longer. There was no way Allana would be merciful, not after he took something she found so precious away from her,especially in the way he did. He felt as if he would explode. He made a mistake. A huge mistake. He needed more time to get prepared. Then maybe he could learn how to use his newly found power he felt he deserved.

All the lies he had been hiding behind slowly seemed to crumble in front of him. He couldn't possibly be the strongest alive while Allana was still breathing. She had to die. She had to. But he couldn't defeat her all alone, not now. Not anymore. The previous May Queen was ancient and tired, she'd barely put up a fight. Allana on the other hand, she was young and he had just killed her friend, a dearly loved friend judging from the copious amount of tears. He felt sweat trickle down his forehead as he saw Allana put her hair up. He had to distract her to escape. He needed to run, but then what would people think about him after that? It would destroy him forever.The Hymn grew louder and louder, echoing in his ears. He cursed the Fae under his breath, not just for the defeat she might possibly hand him, but for how easily she'd managed to obtain such strength. Why did he have to work for his power and she didn't have to? *No, this isn't a fair battle. She is too strong. It's not fair. I worked for my power! All of it.* He sucked in a breath. He had nowhere to run, so he straightened himself and prepared to fight.

Chapter Eighteen

Allana glanced at Evan's lifeless body, then back into Verratyrr's smug green eyes. "They raised me when my own kind were too lazy and uncaring to do it themselves." She took a step forward. "I was a stranger and they took me in despite the time, effort, and money I cost them in later years." She took another step, this time he backed away. *You're afraid, that's good.* "They loved me like no one here has ever done. Evan was my best friend, and he paid the ultimate price for me." Now the fear could be seen in his eyes, but pride still outshone it.

"If they mean so much to you, you can go and join them." Snarling, he thrust upward, with his sword. Allana shot her hand forward, closing her eyes. She focused her rage into the palm of her hand, and imagined a leaf, first green, then a canvas of colors, and finally a crumbling heap of dust. She flicked her eyes open.

The tip met her palm, but she followed through with her movement and, as her hand moved forward, the sword disintegrated into ooze until there was nothing left but the red gem that had rested in the cross guard. Veratyrr stumbled backward, and a smirk slid onto Allana's face. She stepped forward and he scrambled in reverse.

"Humans understand that life is precious and short, but our immortality causes us to forget. Our negligence has allowed you to take life whenever you please. I had to learn the hard way that life is precious, and it should be protected, regardless of species. And neither humans nor Fae will die by your hands again." Light filled her heart and shone from within her, casting a golden haze around her figure. But even light can be malefic, and righteous anger blazed across her regal features. The Shadow Court leader had retreated a larger distance, but even from that point he heard her low spoken words.

"You didn't kill some meaningless human, you killed my best friend, and if it's the last thing I do, I. Will. End. You." Her hands rested by her side, and with these words she flicked them forward and clenched them. Her fist loosened considerably as two daggers made of clear ice appeared in her hands. With a guttural yell that echoed throughout the courtyard, she charged forward. A few feet from her opponent she leaped in the air, her new wings giving her extra purchase as she twirled for extra momentum. Her daggers swiped his face in succession but both times a shadowy blade deflected them. She landed on the ground, both feet planted firmly, and thrust herself forward once more. Allana breathed hard, though trained in combat, her opportunity for practical use had been limited, the ground was becoming marshier as they progressed further and further from the Shadow Court stronghold. She threw her daggers, but with a flick of his wrist a shadowy wall intercepted them. She sprang at him again but once her foot hit the ground it was encapsulated in mud and held both her feet captive. Adrenaline coursed through her veins, she tried to struggle but the more she did so the quicker she sank. Veratyrr yawned absentmindedly and drew a boot dagger.

"Even with all that power you're still as unobservant as a child. The magic made a poor choice. But it will choose another very soon." He smirked and advanced painstakingly. *It's him, he's manipulating the ground that's why I'm sinking so fast. Ah, Mud in my leg Ow. I have to get out of this muck.* The mud was up to her thighs now and her hands were covered as well. He was close enough to strike her now. And he smirked, "I'm going to enjoy this." Without wasting any time, he stepped forward to deliver his blow. Taking a deep breath, Allana focused her energy into her hands. The grass beneath her attacker's boots began to die, but Verratyr didn't seem to notice. She closed her eyes, blocking out the pain surging from the innumerable cuts littered across her body.. *Just a little longer.* Thump.. She opened her eyes and saw Verratyr lying on the ground, an odd stunned, fatigued look on his face, dead, brown grass surrounding him.

"I'm not the only one who needs to work on my observation skills." She made blocks of ice under her feet and slowly she ascended out of the mud until she was on solid ground. Stepping next to him, Allana created a sword and prepared to end the pitiful figure below her.

"You won't kill me.You're too weak. Your love of life is too strong. And how could you hurt your best friend?"

"What are you —" Allana gasped, his face morphed and instead of a hard pale gray face, with coal black eyes she saw an innocent teenager with messy brown hair and mismatching eyes. A goofy grin spread across his features.

"Allana. Why are you pointing your sword at me? I—I thought I was your friend now."

Allana's hands trembled. She squeezed her eyes shut. *It's not him, it's not him, Evan's dead, he's in a better place, it's Verratyrr, he's trying to distract you.* The image of Evan's smiling face swam unbidden into mind, and Allana felt her heart clench fiercely. When she opened her eyes, he was still there, with fear in his green and brown irises. She stumbled backwards. *What am I doing? How can I attack him? I know it's not him, I know it can't be him, he was just attacking me. But...* The ice of her sword began to condensate as her hands started to sweat. *Crack!* Her blade slipped from her fingers and shattered against the ground. Evan stood, and a fowl smirk slid across his face. *Evan —* Hot tears welled up in her eyes, threatening to drop, and Evan's twisted grin widened. Her heart plummeted. *There's no way that's him, I saw him get stabbed, but I can't kill him, not him, not like this I —* He began to speak.

"You say that humans are so wonderful, but what will you think of them when the one you trust kills you where you stand?" A howl split the air and instantly six shadow wolves surrounded her. Red eyes glared menacingly and their white teeth were a stark contrast to the black of their body. Allana, her heart pounding, whirled around, looking in turn at their eerily white fangs and beady, crimson irises as they began to circle closer and closer to her, their snarls filling the deathly silent woods. Fighting to keep her composure, Allana wracked her brains for what to do. *I'm not entirely confident with my wings, so if I try to take off, they'll be able to grab me before I can get away for sure. Agh, but how do you fight shadow wolves?* Despite every instinct telling her not to, she risked a look at Veratyrr. Seeing the menacing, mad gleam of the Shadow Court heir's gaze in Evan's once-kind, cheerful eyes was haunting, and she tore her eyes away almost instantly. *Stop being such a coward, it's not him.* One of the larger wolves took a small step closer, baring his jowls wide in a hideous snarl. Allana whirled to face it, and immediately the surrounding shadow creatures growled louder than ever, their wispy, jet-black fur bristling so that they each looked twice as big. In spite of the burning heat of the swamp, a cold chill of unease ran down Allana's spine. *If I attack one of them, all of the others will come for me. They're just waiting for me to snap and attack.* Verratyr was circling the fray along the outside, a dagger gripped tight in his fist. An agonizing pang jolted through Allana's heart as she caught a glance of his vengeful expression across Evan's face. *I wish Evan were here. He might have had some crazy idea-* Suddenly, a memory that felt like it was from eons ago leapt into mind, the image of Gristle being pinned down by the massive bear Evan had dubbed 'Vincent'. *This is absolutely insane, but it just might work.* Dredging up any memories of Spring Court Fae shapeshifting, Allana squeezed her eyes shut and willed the power to come to her. It began to spread from her fingertips throughout her whole body, and for a moment she had the strange sensation that she had vanished. *Oh gosh, I really wished I'd asked Thea more about how to shapeshift. Think bear…* The peculiar feeling of being stretched filled her, along with an odd, sunny feeling, and suddenly, she felt her feet strike the ground. Blinking open her eyes, Allana was suddenly aware of how much taller she was.

She glanced down to see a pair of massive, hairy paws and a thick, wooly coat. *It worked!* Glancing over her shoulder, she watched as the wolves backed away, their tails tucked slightly and their posture hunched. The large wolf that had advanced earlier, however, strode forward, and gave an ear-splitting howl. The surrounding wolves, in spite of their obvious fear, lunged forward.

Allana felt agony shoot through one of her legs as one of the canines buried its fangs deep into it, and gave a yelp of pain. However, the sound came out as a fearsome bellow that rang through the cypress trees that caused the surrounding wolves to leap back, their eyes wide. Bearing her teeth, Allana lunged forward and took a massive swipe with one of her brutal paws. She stumbled as her weight came down on one of her forelegs, but her blow hit home. One of the shadow wolves was sent flying through the air with a high- pitched yelp of terror and pain. It crashed down into the grass, poofing away into nothing more than dark smoke upon impact.

Allana only had a moment to take in her victory when she felt a weight hit her back, and felt teeth grasp the back of her neck. Growling furiously, she reared again, shaking her head, but the creature refused to let go. Out of the corner of her eye, she saw another of the canines prepare to leap for her head, and swung it out of the way just in time. She slammed a paw down on top of the creature with all of the force she could muster, and watched as it too vanished into ebony whisps. She felt teeth fasten themselves onto the back of one of her hindlegs, and another pair snapped themselves onto one of her ears. She snarled, trying once more to rear, but the pressure on the back of her neck from the wolf's jaws was making her feel weak and fuzzy-headed. Blinking back the fogginess, she spotted the nearby trunk of an ancient dead cypress, and an idea burst into mind. Summoning up all of the strength she could, she lurched toward it, ramming her shoulders into it. Pain from the blow jolted through her, and she could feel her mouth filling with blood from where she'd bitten her tongue, but the wolf's hold on her neck was released, and she watched as the creature sank slowly to the ground and vanished like its comrades. Stepping back from the trunk, Allana paused to take in who was left. The three remaining wolves were once again circling, led by the larger one who commanded them. *Wait. Where did Verratyr go?* Her thoughts were interrupted as the two smaller wolves lunged both at once, slamming into her side. Her breath was driven from her as she hit the ground. Flailing to get up, Allana suddenly found herself peering into the lead wolf's vermilion eyes.

The beast gave a triumphant snarl, evidently savoring the gleeful moment before moving to kill her. Fighting every instinct she possessed, Allana allowed her power to subside, feeling the peculiar stretching feeling come over her once more. The thick, suffocating fur vanished, and she was a Fae again. The wolf, who'd been standing across her fuzzy chest when she'd transformed, stumbled forward as the surface his paws had been standing on vanished.

Without thinking, Allana summoned icicles to her fingertips, flinging them outward toward the wolf, who was spinning around to face her once more. They pierced it's sides, driven deep into its smoky black fur. The creature froze in place, its jaws open in a shocked yelp, before collapsing to the ground to wisp away in a little trail of blackness. Gasping for breath, Allana looked up to see the two remaining wolves peering at the spot where their leader had once been, fearfully.

As she rose to her feet, the two creatures turned and vanished into the shadows of the trees.

Breathing heavily, she searched for her enemy. Her back ached from the scratches the wolves had given her, and blood oozed from her leg and throbbed with a vengeance. Spinning around she looked in the direction of Molderbough, but her adversary was nowhere to be seen. *You should call for him. Yeah because he's going to answer. The only reason he would answer is if he attained more than just Evan's looks in his creepy transformation.* Shuddering tensely at the thought, she trudged towards the castle, hoping to escape the stifling atmosphere of the humid woodland.

"Allana." She spun around, but only trees filled her vision.

"Where are you?" Allana muttered, and spun in a slow circle.

"Where do you think I am?" It was Evan's voice that spoke, but it had a menacing prideful edge that showed that Verratyr was the one behind it. *You can't see him, he's using the shadows, just stay where you are and listen; he'll reveal his position, you just have to pay attention.* Taking a deep breath, she stood still, feet together, eyes closed, ears perked for the slightest noise. But, despite her concentration, no out of the ordinary sound permeated the silence of the woods. She wanted to sit to rest her burning leg, and sweat trickled down her back. *Crack.* She flicked her eyes open and looked around, but nothing was there. She looked down and stifled a groan. In her nervousness she had frozen her hands again, and it was the ice that had cracked so loudly. In the heat the fallen ice melted rapidly and she watched it vanish. *Why isn't he doing anythi-* Pain erupted in her side, and her feet left the ground. Her stomach churned ominously and her back seemed to scream in pain as she slammed into a tree,

"Ahg!" she took a sharp breath, her back arched and her neck snapped backwards, twisting painfully. Vaguely she was aware that she was sitting and that someone was standing in front of her. Blinking, she saw Evan's kind face peering down at her. *Evan's here, maybe I'm dead. But I can't be dead, that means Verratyr is alive, and if I'm dead that means he won, maybe I should ask.*

"Am I dead?" she wondered.

"No, but you will be very very soon." He had a dagger in his hand and he moved his arm back, poised to strike, his mouth slowly turning into a malevolent smile. She had just enough time to think, *that's not Evan,* before lunging to her right and crawling away, the blade just managing to swipe her arm. *Good thing it wasn't Nulada, or I'd be dead. Ugh I could really use a magic sword right now.* Thorns pricked her hands and knees, her whole body gnawed with pain. She could hear Verratyr behind her. Desperately, Allana tried to calm her frantic mind down so that she could come up with a plan. In her attempt to placate her frazzled mind a comforting image came unbidden to the front of her brain. *A long, thin sword of bright gold with a cheerful, flower- covered hilt sat upon a shelf above the stag, its immaculate patterns and unnatural sheen drawing the eye. The sword! I can make that, I just have to buy myself time.* With this realization she began to flap her wings and slowly she rose from the ground, Moving forward, she sped through the trees, zigzagging haphazardly in an attempt to confuse her rapidly gaining nemesis. Her lungs were burning agonizingly from the effort of trying to stay ahead of her assailant, and her wings felt like they might fall off from the speed she was flapping them. *I'm injured and exhausted. There is absolutely no way I'll be able to outrun him.* A sharp crackling nearly made her plummet out of the sky in fear, and she glanced rapidly down to see tiny fragments of frost flying from her fingertips. *That's it! I'll –* "*Ow!*" She yelled in pain as her wing caught a cluster of thin, leafy branches, sending her plummeting several feet into the marshy ground below.

Gasping and wheezing for breath, Allana wiped droplets of mud from her eyes and stumbled to her feet, surprised to find that her landing left her no worse for the wear. *I didn't think I could ever be grateful for this soft, marshy ground, yet here we are.* She could see Verratyr weaving through the trees, coming closer and closer. Summoning her Winter Court power, Allana directed her hand toward a patch of wetness on the forest floor and pulled up. Icy walls rose rapidly from the moist earth, rising higher and higher until they enveloped the weak shafts of sunlight poking through the thick canopy, blocking her into a frigid box of ice. Concentrating, she thought about what the May queen had told her.

'Each May Queen's sword is different, but it combines the powers of all four seasons into one. For me, the opposite of my birth court is Autumn so when I made mine, I started with a funnel of wind as a core, and slowly built upon the same concept. Next was Winter and so on. But the design and the look of the sword is completely different, no sword looks the same and the way it operates is always slightly different.' Well here goes, Summer first. Allana concentrated, summer was her opposite and using their magic would be the hardest for her. She closed her eyes, and spread her fingers apart, trying to remember what Athena had told her about Summer court magic. Slowly, she pressed her spread fingers together and carefully inched them away from each other. Her muscles buzzed with energy, as she thought about Rosela's sword, about her crown and how vines weaved around each of those sacred objects. *Tick, tick,tick,tick,* Allana opened her eyes, He was there, a Shadowy pick tapping away at her fortress of ice. A scowl covered Evan's features, her concentration broke and the buzz began to fade as fear crept through her, but she shook her head. *I have to do this, what Evan did for you means nothing if you hesitate.* She closed her eyes again and twisted her hands, and instinct took over. She opened her eyes and focused on her creation, a thin vine of yellow energy hung in the air, pink and blue zinnias blossomed from the vine, and a hot tear slid down her face. *I should have let him enjoy those flowers for as long as he could. He was so emphatic about them, and they weren't even for him. They*

were for his family. Tick tick tick tick. She looked at her opponent again, and ice erupted from her fingers covering the vine in clear sharp ice. How *dare you defile Evan's appearance, and pretend to be him in any way.* She re-focused on her creation that now resembled a sword, the cold of the hilt froze her hand, and with a final burst of power she covered the hilt with petrified cherry wood, the outline of maple leaves imprinted into it. Verratyr was almost through the ice. *Let him come.* She flicked her wrist and the ice walls dissipated.

"You think another one of your handmade swords is going to stop me?" He laughed but Allana didn't waste her time. *You are a slimy coward hiding behind the image of everything you wish you could be. And I will tolerate it no longer.*

She roared, and charged. No longer did the fear of hurting what looked like her friend hold her back. In the fraction of a second that Verratyr's eyes met hers, she saw no trace of the kind-eyed friend who'd been willing to defend her when nobody else would, who'd been her friend even when she was unkind to him, who'd understood when nobody else seemed to. Driving the blade forward with all of the strength she had, she rammed it deep into Verratyr's abdomen. As the sword met his body, the illusion he'd wrapped himself in faded and Verratyr, tyrant leader of the Shadow Court, returned just long enough to register his death. He gawked at Allana, shock widening his sickly green eyes. Then, her sword pulsed with energy and the vine within it glowed until the light burst from the tip and disintegrated the late leader of the Shadow Court Fae.

Allana watched as the fragments of light, the only thing left of the tyrannical Fae, drifted into nothingness, the cogs within her mind slowly taking it all in. She was only hazily cognizant of dropping to her knees as her exhausted and battered legs gave out beneath her. She peered up at the shafts of sunlight beaming through the thinning trees and upon her dust and blood stained face.

"It's all over," she murmured aloud, tilting her face upward. "Evan, Thea, Rosela... We won."

Epilogue

As she went up the steps towards the throne that her predecessor— her friend— had sat in, she felt her heart racing. She knew she would have many new responsibilities, but now she felt like she could handle them. It was like a huge weight had been lifted off of her shoulders. She could finally breathe. She stepped onto the ground right below the gold throne and observed it. The newly polished throne rested beneath a golden frame, delicately carved flowers littering the surface. She sat down and looked around, thinking about her new responsibility. The duties of a Queen were numerous but she was proud of how she had handled the Shadow Court after Verratyrr's defeat. Once she had been instated as Queen, she'd had a visit from the new Shadow Court leader, Gaelin. After a long discussion of events, they proposed a treaty and the negotiations were still in progress. Thinking of Gaelin's story made her reminisce. How dearly she missed Evan. *He would have ogled over this room.* She smiled sadly. For a few weeks Allana had pondered what she would tell Evan's parents. She refused to remove all memory of him from their minds, even after everything Evan had done for them, Hyacinth's ideas about human interaction were still incredibly flawed, and this suggestion had been one of many. Even with her experience with them, none of the Courts knew enough about humans to come up with a convincing lie to tell the parents. Finally, she had settled on the truth. She had walked to their door and performed many magical feats before they finally believed her. Once the truth had been revealed they had set up a wonderful weekend treat for her and she couldn't wait for them to arrive. They were devastated of course, but they were proud of how he had conducted himself and were happy that Allana was doing okay. They were so upset, it made Allana tense up. *I'm so sorry, guys.* She wished it could have been different. Tallula slowly walked into the room, tail between her legs. She looked up at Allana and in her very squeaky, high pitched voice she said, "Allana! Noel and Vincent are here to see you!"

Right after she heard what Tallula had to say, she got up, not questioning how they got here. She felt herself smile. What a joy it would be to see these two. As Tallula was guiding her towards them she kept thinking about all of the very long, considerate talks she had with Evan. Every word she had said to him. Every time she laughed with him. She wasn't ready to say goodbye and neither was anyone else. She wondered how Vincent and Noel felt about this. She knew that Evan's parents hadn't initially believed anything about Aeternum and Evan's death, and that made complete sense. A world different from theirs didn't or wouldn't make sense to any human so it was hard for them to grasp at first. She hoped they found comfort in knowing that their son was a friend and hero to the Fae.

She walked out of the room and saw a tiny girl dressed in overalls with a pink bucket hat with green polka dots on it. Noel turned her way and smiled, running towards her. Allana also sped up and just as Noel got to her, Allana picked her up and held her. Noel was hugging her so tightly, it made her feel warm inside. "I miss Evan."

"I know. I do too." She felt herself tearing up, but she couldn't possibly cry in front of Noel. She felt bad but of course she knew Noel was very strong. *She's also too young to understand.*

While hugging her tightly, Allana noticed something in the corner of her eye. *Vincent!* He walked up, as if he was shy and Allana put Noel down and reached out to pet him. "Hi Vincent," she said.

Hello, The bear's low rumbling reply echoed in her head, *how are you faring?*

"Well enough," muttered Allana, looking away as the black bear's beady black eyes bore meaningfully into her. "And you?"

As well as I can be. The huge beast gave a little shake of his shaggy head. *I miss him dearly, though.*

Allana swallowed the lump rising in her throat. "So do I." She glanced down at the little girl trying to clamber her way onto Vincent's shoulders. "I think he would be beyond happy to know that you've struck up a friendship with his little sister."

The bear gave an amused grunt, nudging the little girl supportively as she finally managed to haul herself up on top of him. "I'm on top of the world!" squealed Noel excitedly, lifting her arms with a wide grin on her face.

Allana smiled. She really was such a sweet soul. After playing around for a bit, Allana asked them if they would like to go see the throne. She led them to the room and as soon as the door opened, Noel, while on Vincent, struggled to get off his back but made it to the floor and came running up to Allana on the throne. Allana grabbed her and put her on her lap. She giggled and it made Allana laugh a bit. She noticed how much Noel reminded her of Evan. Her smile, her laugh, even the way she talked. Evan always seemed like he wasn't paying attention, which was true for the most part. But when Allana forgot something important, Evan always remembered. It always amazed her. She wondered what she would say to him if it were her last conversation with Evan.

After a few hours of nonsense, Tallula came to get Vincent and Noel and went home. Allana sat down on the throne with some paper and a writing utensil. She decided to write a note. A note to Evan as if he were still here, right by her side.

Dear Evan, I miss you. I miss laughing and talking with you. You were such a great friend and an even better person. I wish

you didn't have to leave us because you didn't deserve to. Tell me, how were you so strong? I know you didn't want to die, but how could you be so strong in the face of death? I can't possibly understand, or comprehend anything that has happened. I wish I could have watched you experience the rest of this world. You were one of my dearest friends and I don't think any of us wanted to lose you so early. I've never really had a friendship like yours, and I know that if you were here you would say that wasn't true, but it is... I wanted to apologize for whenever I pushed you away, but I couldn't speak the right words, and now I'll never have a chance. I'm sorry. I will never forget what you did for me, and for my world, so I guess the only thing left for me to say is this.. Thank you, Evan, for everything.
    -Allana

Tear stains dotted the paper as she finished, folded it up, and put it in her backpack. She didn't know where she would send this to or who to send it to but she knew that if Evan were here, he would probably smile and then give her a big hug. She got up and decided to check in the room where she would now be living. She walked to the room and opened the door, feeling her heart clench. She could remember many days spent with the Queen in her quarters, helping her prepare for cordial events as they bantered and talked about life. Even now, after being redecorated to fit the current Queen, the place still felt like a second home to her. *I wonder if Rosela is proud of me,* she thought. As she passed by the dresser and the mirror that Rosela had often stood before, she noticed a letter lying on its surface. Picking it up, she tore it gingerly open, and pulled out the neatly folded piece of paper inside.

    Dear Allana, you and Evan are heroes to us. We don't know how we could ever possibly repay you. We shall never forget. - Your fellow Fae
    They didn't say thank you, how rude. She laughed at herself. *I'll just have to start telling people to say it, if I don't I'll*

While holding the note in her hand, she went to the window and looked out to see different colored trees swaying in a huge field. She knew she needed to protect the one thing she saved. She felt proud of herself. She didn't want to live for other people from now on. She didn't want to try to live up to her parents expectations. No, not anymore. She could create her own future for herself. She wanted to make her own decisions based on what she thought was right instead of based on what others thought of her, but before she could do that she needed to go to the funeral for Evan. His parents wanted to have one and they invited her to come along because they knew Evan was her friend. She hadn't really known his parents that long but she knew that they had been grateful towards her. She felt a sharp twinge of guilt twist her heart. How could they possibly be grateful towards her? Their son had given his life to protect her. If anything she should be grateful that they raised their son to be such an amazing person. She decided she would give his parents the note. Maybe to keep for themselves, maybe to hang up somewhere in their house. She didn't know what she would possibly say to them when giving it to them but she knew she wanted to give it to them as a present. She hoped they could all get to know each other a little better. After all, she was now friends with Noel and Vincent.

She set the letter down and realized she should prepare for the funeral tomorrow. She decided she would wear a dress. She hadn't worn one in weeks. *It would be the most appropriate thing for his funeral.* It was still weird to have the Fae she had previously worked with under her command. She dug out a dress that she hoped would be suitable, setting it aside for the next day. She felt tired, very tired. She went back to the bed, yawned and crawled under the sheets. For the first time in a long time she could sleep. Possibly because she was laying on a real bed with a pillow and she wasn't in a dark forest with no food or light. *Man, it feels good to finally not sleep on the hard rock floor with no blanket.* But then again, she would rather sleep on the hard rock floor and have no pillow if it meant Evan was still here.

After a peaceful night, the sun rose up. Allana got up and stretched her arms. She quickly prepared for the funeral, taking care to tuck her wings securely away from sight.

Once she was all ready she headed for the nearest ring that would bring her to the human world. Evan's parents wanted to have the funeral where Evan's grandfather was. She found that very sweet in a way. After getting dropped off at the funeral home, she entered the building to find many solemnly dressed people milling about.

"Hey, Allana." The Fae whirled around to see Evan's mother approaching her, a weak smile on her face.

"Oh, hi." She smiled.

"I was wondering if you would possibly want to give a speech for Evan? It would mean so much if you did. Obviously you don't have to but—"

"Oh. Of course! Yes, yes! I'll do it."

"Thank you, I know, I know it's a lot to ask. You've been so patient explaining the real facts about- about my son's death. And-" Evan's mom broke down. Allana was unsure what to do. It had taken a few days for Evan's parents to even speak to Allana after she explained the situation. She understood that. Yet, somehow they had begun to be sweet to her and had invited her to dinner on several occasions. She wanted to give Mrs. Hale a hug, but she wasn't sure whether it would be a welcome gesture. After a few moments, the distraught mother collected herself.

"I'll just tell you when you have to go up. You don't have to prepare. Just say anything you want."

"Alright, thank you." Allana sat down on a bench where some of Evan's young relatives sat. Noel came running up to her and hugged her legs. Allana hugged Noel, who was crying. She probably didn't understand what was going on. It hurt her heart to see Noel like this. "H-hey, Allana!" She wiped her tears away and smiled. It was so amazing how little children could become so happy even after crying only a minute before. She wondered if she was ever like that. Maybe when she was younger. "Please sit with me!"

"Okay, I will."

Noel led her to a bench close to the front. Pictures of Evan hung from the walls above. There was one stage and a microphone on it. There was no casket. Even so, they still wanted to celebrate Evan's life and so did she.

As people went up to give speeches about how they met Evan or who he was to them, Allana rehearsed her speech in her brain. She knew exactly what she wanted to say. She was ready. She couldn't focus on the person speaking, and she didn't know why. While thinking, she glanced at Evan's mother who met her gaze. She mouthed the words *go ahead,* and gave her a watery smile. Allana got up from the bench and made her way up to the stage where every eye was on her. She didn't mind though. As everyone was looking her way, she leaned into the microphone.

"These past few days have been a struggle for me. Evan was someone who changed my life forever. I remember this one time I was talking to him and," she felt tears roll down her cheek and wiped them away with a handkerchief from the back pocket of the dress, "He told me something that has stuck with me through it all. He told me that people may forget what you said but will never forget how you made them feel. He was such a kind soul. Please understand how much he did for everyone and everything. He always saw the good in people. Sometimes when I feel down, I try to think of what Evan would have done. He was always positive and he was very bright. He was very passionate about helping others, not even the tiniest ant in distress, escaped his notice, and that's what made him so special. He was such a good friend to me even in times of anger, he was soft towards anyone and everyone. He always made me laugh even though I tend to be very negative. We were polar opposites in some ways but we clicked, which I don't understand, but that was the joy of it all. He always surprised me. He will be missed. By all of us. Thank you." Silent tears leaked from her eyes as she walked back to her seat.

The next person went up. Wiping her tears away, she sat down. Allana got up to leave, a sudden exhaustion taking over her. Allana realized Noel was looking at her. Just as she pulled the door open to leave, Evan's mom grabbed her hand and Noel clutched her legs. Allana looked back at her to see tears in their eyes. Mrs. Hale then hugged Allana tightly, just like Noel. "T-thank you."

"You're welcome," she said as they let go and began walking away, when she remembered.

"Wait," she turned around. "I— I thought you might want to have this." She held out Evan's necklace, and watched as Mrs. Hale's jaw dropped. "I-I thought Noel might want to have it maybe when she's old enough to understand." Allana trailed off looking at the ground. Arms enveloped her and soon she was in Mrs. Hale's long comforting embrace.

"Thank you," Evan's mother whispered. Then, pulling away, she opened her purse and retrieved a small manilla envelope and forced it into Allana's hands. "You don't have to open it right away, I know you have a slew of responsibilities to get back to." Allana's throat caught so she nodded gratefully before walking out. She felt bad for leaving so soon but she needed to go back to the castle. She needed to escape the words she just managed to put into place. How did she come up with that at such short notice? She would never know. She started to walk away.

After arriving at the castle she headed to her quarters to change. As she took off the dress and got into a shirt and jeans, she thought about Evan's mom's eyes. They really did look similar to Evan's except for the fact that he had one green eye and his mom did not. How she longed to see Evan's eyes. They were beautiful after all. She unlocked the bathroom and went back into her room in the castle. She was exhausted but she didn't know why. She was too tired to sleep. Maybe she was tired from all of this. It really was a crazy journey. Sitting on her bed, she opened the envelope Mrs. Hale had given her. Allana gasped. Inside was a standard sized photograph of Evan grinning widely, probably due to the snowy landscape that surrounded him. A hot tear dripped off her chin. For a long time all she could do was sit and stare into his big brown eyes, and the joy and wonder the photo had so perfectly captured. *You really were like another family to me. And I know just where to put you.* Wiping her eyes, Allana went over to an ornately carved shelf and pulled out a beautiful but worn scrapbook. Flipping to the last page she slipped it onto a page with a picture of her and Jay in the snow. *What do you know, you fit right in.* Allana let out a watery chuckle before laying the book on the bed.

She had gained and lost, but she would never go back. She could only go forward from here. She felt her head throb. She looked down at her leg and sighed with relief.

Allana got up and looked out of the window once again. Something about the outside made her want to go save the world again. She suddenly felt invincible like all of her fears were irrelevant, that no matter what anybody said to her she would think of her past with happiness, and treasure her memories with Evan with equal fondness. How she had waited forever to feel this feeling. She smiled. She couldn't wait for all of the things she would do. She knew she needed to get to work but on what? Where to start? *I know I can't lead all on my own, of course. I shouldn't think like that anymore.* Leading everyone wasn't going to be easy. There would be a ton more journeys she would have to make. A ton of losses she would have to deal with and a ton of things she could potentially gain. She needed to go back to Athena and see her again. She needed to see her friends. She wanted the support of her friends instead of relying on only herself. She wanted to learn things; lessons. She couldn't point her finger at it exactly. As much as she wanted to give up on it, Evan was always positive and that made her feel like she shouldn't give up. She was sure he wanted to give up too but he never seemed to show it at all. It made her curious as to how he was so positive. She wanted to be exactly like that. Positive.

She had a whole life full of duties and lessons to learn waiting for her. She grabbed her bag and went outside. She wanted to observe more. She saw Evan everywhere but it didn't make her sad, no, it made her happy. Maybe this was his sign that he was still here. That's how she would want to think about it. She gently touched the bullets on the chain Evan's parents had allowed her to keep, a permanent reminder of her heroic friend. Now she could finally go on without worrying that she didn't get to say everything she wanted to before he was gone. She felt like he already knew everything she wanted to say in that note. The thought made her smile.

Pronunciation Guide

Aeternum: A - tear - noom

Hestflue: Hest - flew

Skynjari: Skin - jar - ee

Tablarye: Tab - lar - rye

Veratyrr: V - air - uh - tear

About the Authors

My name is Kelly Beilfuss, and I am a 17-year-old junior in high school. I am a bookworm whose other pastimes include drawing, horseback riding, and overthinking absolutely everything. I had a blast during my second year in this class and learned a ton about writing and plotting a good book along the way. Thanks guys, for the wonderful year!

My name is Lydia Freeman, I am fifteen and this is my third time writing for this class. Hmmm, things you should know about me.. I love classic literature and have recently finished reading A.C. Doyle's complete Sherlock Holmes collection, which I absolutely loved. I live on a twenty three acre farm which is useful because the large yard allows me to practice my KMMA (Krav Maga Martial Arts) forms without hindrance. Oh! And as you can probably see from my Belle dress, I also love making costumes and going to Comic-Con to hang out with all my fellow nerds.

Hi, I'm Chloe. A little bit about me. I'm 15, I like to skateboard, and I love music.

Thank you so much for supporting our students with your purchase of this book.
All proceeds go toward future Class Source scholarships.

If you would like to find out more about the Class Source Novel class and see updates on future projects, visit us on Facebook and Instagram.
@ClassSourceNovel
https://www.facebook.com/ClassSourceNovel
https://www.instagram.com/classsourcenovel/

If you have any questions or comments you would like to share with the student authors, please feel free to email us at
classsourcenovel@gmail.com.

Thank you for reading!